FIRST TILT

BROKEN LANCES

BOOK 0.5

LUCIEN BURR

SH BOOKS

FIRST TILT

Broken Lances 0.5

by Lucien Burr

Published by SH Books

Edited by Drew McBlain

Cover art by M. Lopez, @martes_con_m

Category (Adult Fiction)

Genre (Romance/ Fantasy / Sports / LGBT)

* * *

This content includes, but is not limited to:

Violence, swearing, nudity, explicit homosexual sexual content, injury, classism, sexism

1
ALARIC

The tournament grounds were worn thin by the time Isembard Alaric Blackmere arrived. What lush fields he had pictured in his daydreams lay pressed into mud; the banners, once bright with heraldry, now clung to their poles like sullied rags. A week's worth of tramping feet had sucked the life from this place, and even the promise of sport sagged beneath the weight of a season nearly spent.

Not exactly the fanfare of courtly lists he'd longed for, but what else could he expect from provincial entertainment? Still, Alaric had resolved to taste every rung of glory, even if it meant stooping to these backwater theatrics.

He dismounted at the fringe of merchants' stalls, where greasy pies and sun-bleached leather vied for buyers. No one spared him a glance, and that suited him fine. Only Fiona, his prize mare, drew attention. Even beneath the dust of travel, Fiona's noble breeding shone through her silver-grey coat, dappled elegantly at the haunches. She stood a full hand taller than most warhorses, her silken mane cascading down her powerful neck.

Alaric caught a stable hand's stare; the boy's obvious surprise buckling beneath years of servitude until it settled into a more polite interest. Well. Bringing her had been a risk. She was a tell.

Still, he decided, let them look. So long as he was here, he was no one of importance.

He led the mare through the outer ring of activity, past vendors hawking dubious meat pies and leather goods of various quality. A child darted past, clutching a wooden sword that Alaric judged to be poorly balanced even for a toy. Two squires argued over a water bucket, their voices sharp with exhaustion—had their knights not taught them proper decorum? Disorder pressed in from all sides. Alaric's hand tightened on the reins, a reflex ingrained—a faintly haughty recoil from disorder, from the suggestion of squalor. Late season always looked like this, with all the glamour stripped away. But he' d wanted this challenge, hadn't he? To prove himself where no one knew his name or bloodline. He would simply have to endure the filth like a commoner.

The knights who lingered so late in the season fell into two kinds: those too successful to bother leaving, and those too desperate to afford quitting. The first would be complacent. The second would be reckless.

Both, Alaric decided, would make worthy opponents to fall before his lance.

The registration pavilion squatted near the main lists, its yellow canvas patched so many times it looked threadbare, the pennant hanging limp in the fetid heat. The reek of horse dung clung to every beam, and mud caked the ground where rough knights had dragged their mounts. For the gods' sake, what a mess. Alaric had to school his breathing as he drew close.

Inside, a scribe sat slumped behind a wooden table, his ledger and quill shoved carelessly aside. He was gaunt and dark-eyed, worn down to the point that Alaric would scarcely have blinked if the man expired on the spot.

Alaric braced himself against the stink, fingers curled around the pommel of his sword in silent disgust. The scribe didn't even glance up. When Alaric cleared his throat, the man's lip curled as if the sight of polished armour and spotless surcoat nauseated him.

"Registration closed three days past," the scribe drawled. "Brackets are set."

Alaric halted before the desk and waited. Silence stretched between them, broken only by the scribe's fingers, drumming their irritation into the table. But Alaric was a creature of court, and waiting games were the least taxing of courtly melodrama. This miserable clerk would wilt first.

And indeed he did.

When the man glanced up, his anger immediately thawed into something more cautious as he took in Alaric's polished armour and the high-bred mare stamping just outside.

"Closed. . ." the clerk repeated, the word trailing off as if he weren't quite convinced.

Alaric forced a courteous smile and made sure his voice came out steady. Cordial, even. Just how he was raised.

"I've ridden since before dawn to compete here. I'd hate to see all that effort go to waste."

"Rules are rules, ser. The marshal—"

"—Isn't here," Alaric interrupted, nodding at the vacant chair. "Unless he's turned invisible. In which case, you've greater problems than late entries."

The scribe's lips twitched. No laughter followed.

Provincial scum. Alaric's jaw ached from maintaining his amicable smile. "Very well," he said, inclining his head again. "If he's merely not present, then you have discretion."

"Do I now?" The scribe's lips twitched. Alaric watched the man's expression flicker: irritation, assessment, recognition that this stranger might be worth the trouble, and finally—there—the flicker of opportunity.

"Entry fee's five silver. Non-negotiable."

Five silver? Preposterous. Five silver could buy the entire pathetic pavilion and the scribe along with it, for all that knave was worth. The weasel thought himself clever. How quaint.

"Of course." Alaric kept his voice level; it took far more to rankle him, after all. He upended his pouch, slowly counting out seven silver coins onto the desk, so the scribe might count along with each clink. "Five for entry. Two for your. . .*discretion*."

The scribe's hand covered the coins before the last one stopped spinning.

"Name and house?"

"Alaric. No house. I'm competing without heraldry."

The scribe's quill paused. His throat bobbed.

Alaric stared down at him, daring him to question further. This kind of thing happened, sometimes bastards seeking glory, disgraced knights chasing redemption, third sons with nothing to inherit and everything to prove. He could pretend to be any one of those men, and none of those roles would fit quite right. Except he was, today, one of the nameless knights. In its own way, that caste was as much a tradition at these tournaments as the great houses' champions.

"A problem, scribe?" Alaric murmured.

The scribe hesitated. Finally, he shrugged.

"The Nameless Knight, then." The scribe's voice went high, brows dancing up his forehead as he made a mark in his ledger. Alaric's gaze narrowed. Was that judgement, from the man who'd just happily accepted a bribe? The insolence made his jaw clench.

"You'll be assigned to whatever bracket has a gap. No complaints if you draw the Upstart first round."

Alaric's expression remained impassive, but an excited jolt quickened his pulse. "Who?"

The scribe nodded toward the main lists, where a distant roar of approval was building. "See for yourself."

The stands, meant for thrice today's rabble, yawned half-empty beneath the blazing sun. A handful of self-important minor lords huddled under patched awnings; off-duty knights, pampered squires, and gentry milled below. No true powerbroker bothered to grace this spectacle— the province's High Lord likely hadn't even noticed the farce unfolding on his land.

The field north of the lists held the real audience, all crammed against the rail: filthy commoners whose stench rose like a miasma from the hot press of bodies. They were utterly uncaring about being doused in the dust rising from the field. Their hoots and vulgar taunts rattled the air, but their racket meant little to someone of quality. The knights preparing in the lists paid them no heed, either.

Alaric found a position at the edge of the field, just meters from the registration pavilion, where a weathered support beam offered something to lean against. From here, the joust appeared in profile: the knights would charge parallel to his sight line, the point of their impact partially obscured by the corner of the stands and the dust that rose in clouds from the trampled earth. But if he craned just right, he could see both the knights perfectly.

The first contestant radiated noble polish–exemplar posture, his weight centred, lance angled precisely as he was no doubt taught by his expensive tutors. His immaculate armour caught the sunlight, heraldry rendered in crimson and gold—the trappings of a lesser noble house's expendable son. House Pidon, Alaric thought it was. He'd serve as a tolerable exercise, but hardly a true challenge.

But the other man—

Alaric studied him.

He rode with a rider's instinct, not a pupil's caution. Pale skin reddening at the neck, he moved as if born in the saddle. It was the easy familiarity of someone who'd learned to ride before he learned to read, if he'd learned to read at all. All that bobbing and swaying and moving with the horse was dangerous; you couldn't let your mount think it had any control.

No master-at-arms worth his salt would permit such carefree sway.

His armour had seen more use than care. Which was more the squire's fault, Alaric supposed—though some knights made it very difficult for their squires to do their jobs well. Dents in the cuirass had been beaten smooth rather than replaced, scratches left to gather their own history. The leather was dark with age and sweat, not the patina of fashion but of long service endured. It was service, Alaric thought, that explained the man's face as well: he had a crooked nose, one that had been broken and set poorly. So many nobles wanted to preserve their faces, regardless of how pretty they were. This man didn't mind appearing a brute.

His reddish-blond hair fell wild at his collar, defying all noble grooming. His ears protruded, and they were red, too, likely from time spent squashed beneath his helmet. But even at a glance, Alaric could tell he was well-muscled. Solid. Beneath every seam and plate, the man was coiled like a spring.

When his squire hefted a battered shield emblazoned in yellow-and-blue—the Upstart's colours—Alaric felt something akin to anticipation. A house so minor he could barely recall its name had plucked him from obscurity. He would cling to this chance with everything he possessed.

A commoner, yes—but potentially the fiercest adversary in this sorry pageant. Far more alluring than any pampered scion in gilded plate.

Alaric adjusted his stance, shoulders squared. Let the real contest begin.

When they finished getting ready, and both knights were properly attired, the herald's trumpet sounded. Both knights spurred their mounts, closing the distance between them in a thunder of hooves. Immediately, it didn't go as Alaric had suspected—the polished knight's lance, for all his training, wavered. He dropped his lance too low, then wobbled with the sudden change in his centre of balance.

The Upstart kept charging. His entire body moved as a single unit: arm, shoulder, seat, horse, all aligned along a trajectory as inevitable as Alaric's next drawn breath.

Bang.

The polished knight left his saddle with a sound like a barrel breaking. He hit the barrier, bounced, and went still in the dust. His horse cantered on, confused, until a handler caught its reins.

The Upstart didn't look back. He completed his pass, slowed to a walk, and raised his visor.

The crowd went wild for him, all of them chanting that strange epithet. *Up-start! Up-start! Up-start!*

The Upstart's square jaw twinged as he offered them all a lopsided smile. He waved at the crowd, then began to beat his breast and hoot. The common folks went wild at this, and ah, no wonder he was a crowd favourite. He was one of their ilk. The Upstart had given them something to believe in: a man like them, risen through merit, defeating the sons of houses who'd never worked for anything. And he wasn't particularly handsome, either, not in the courtly sense—not so unattainably pretty a lowborn schmuck couldn't pretend to be him in his dreams. But certainly, the knight was compelling. And he had all his teeth, which put him far above plenty in that caste.

Interesting.

But there was something else, too. Something in the set of those shoulders, the angle of that head, the sheer breadth of that childish grin. He was prideful but scared. Pride was his real armour, worn over some wound.

Alaric knew exactly what that was like.

———

The scribe was still at his desk when Alaric returned, though the ledger had been nudged aside to make room for an oozing meat pie that looked well on its way to rotting. Gods, the things these people allowed into their bodies.

Suppressing his gorge, Alaric nodded back towards the lists. "Tell me about the Upstart."

The scribe glanced up, still chewing. "What's to tell? Common-born. Born into servitude to some lord. Got his spurs in a border skirmish—saved the lord's son, supposedly. Story shifts, depending on who's telling it." He swallowed. "Been riding the circuit three seasons. Hasn't lost in. . . eighteen months, give or take."

"Eighteen months," Alaric repeated.

"Could be more." The scribe took another bite. "Hard to say. Point is, everyone bets on him. Odds are miserable, but he wins. Crowd eats that up. They like a nobody who keeps coming out on top."

Yes, well, they would, wouldn't they? Alaric suspected he already knew the next question, but he still asked, "Who trains him?"

"Himself, near as anyone can tell. He's got a squire—skinny thing, been with him since the beginning. That's it. No master-at-arms. His patron is some woman, House Kerran, I think. But they're local and upstarts themselves. So it's mostly just him and the boy and whatever coin he wins."

Alaric let the picture settle. He had been right. This man had no lineage to lean on. No instruction to follow but what he'd learned himself. All alone—how had he got started? An image came to Alaric, then, of the Upstart as a boy, falling again and again off his horse, and not giving up. Now he was a man shaped by repetition and reward and awarded a knighthood for all his effort.

Yes, certainly, that kind of man would be rather protective of his title.

Alaric swallowed. So. He had wanted a challenge.

He turned back toward the lists. Through the crowd, he could see the Upstart dismounting, already surrounded by noise and motion. A smaller figure moved to meet him—slight, dark-haired, hands lifting instinctively toward the reins.

The squire from before. He really was a weak-bodied thing.

Alaric watched them.

The Upstart tossed his lance behind him without looking, and the squire's hands were already waiting. The knight stripped his gauntlets and those, too, found their way into the young man's careful grip, tucked under one arm while the other steadied the horse. They moved as one creature with two bodies—knight and squire, master and shadow.

He was too far away to hear, but when the Upstart scolded the squire, the youth's face shuttered. But there was a practice to it that suggested years of such treatment; he took the knight's frustration in stride.

Then the knight came to a sudden stop and turned. His hand fell heavy on the squire's shoulder. To Alaric's eyes, the motion was rough, dismissive even. Yet the squire straightened beneath it like a flower turning towards a harsh sun. Strangely, Alaric's chest tightened at the sight. Here was loyalty in its purest form, the devotion of someone who'd been given purpose in a world that offered little. The squire looked at his knight the way. . . the way, what? Alaric lacked any comparison.

All that unabashed, shameless adoration, and the Upstart didn't even notice. Or perhaps he'd grown so accustomed to that gaze that it had become as invisible as his own shadow.

Alaric swallowed against a sudden dryness in his mouth.

They fit together, those two. Years of shared dust and victory had forged something between them that Alaric couldn't name but suddenly, fiercely wanted.

Brutish, he decided, focusing on the knight again. That

was word for the Upstart. Brutish but brilliant. Someone who would fight Alaric to the last.

A worthy opponent indeed.

And there was the challenge.

Plenty of knights had fallen to him this season. Men clad in finer mail, schooled in loftier academies, born to grander names. They had charged with all the weight their noble houses could muster, and he had dispatched them all to the dust. It was not only objectively impressive, but *interesting.*

He sought the purest test of mettle: skill against skill, unsullied by gilded pedigree or lavish retinue. He was curious, too, to observe how that boastful visage would crumble when confronted with true superiority.

What the proud, brutish face would look like when the Upstart lost.

He returned to the scribe.

"I wish to face the Upstart," he declared.

The scribe set down his meat pie, a glob of glistening animal fat sliding down his chin to join the constellation of grease stains on his tunic. Alaric turned his eyes briefly heavenward as the scribe cleared his throat. "The Upstart?"

Alaric threw out his arms. "Yes! Is there another knight worth facing here?"

The scribe's shrewd gaze measured him again, the faint sparkle of opportunity dawning in his eyes. He leaned back; the chair groaned. "That's not—tournaments are bracketed. You'd have to reshuffle the list. Other riders would need to—"

Oh, for the gods' sake. Did every conversation have to be so irritating? Alaric set more coins on the desk. Copper this time, but more of it. Enough to make the scribe's eyes widen slightly before professional caution reasserted itself.

"The marshal won't like it."

"As if that concerns me," Alaric interrupted, dismissing the objection with a flourish of his hand. "The marshal doesn't need to know. A scheduling error. A clerical mistake. You've been here all season—surely there have been slip-ups."

The scribe's hand crept toward the coins. "There'd need to be a reason. The other competitors—"

"Tell them I demanded it. Tell them I'm a fool. Tell them whatever secures my challenge." Alaric's voice remained pleasant, though fury had built in him. "I didn't ride all this way to watch."

At last, the scribe's fingers closed over the coins.

"Alright. First bout tomorrow morning," he said. "Don't say I didn't warn you."

How amusing. Alaric inclined his head. "You have warned me admirably."

Alaric turned away from the desk.

In the paddock, the Upstart strode toward his tent, scrawny squire lumbering behind him, burdened with helm and gauntlets. The slanted late-day sun cast the knight's silhouette in sharp relief: broad-shouldered, surefooted, carrying that insolent air of entitlement as though the world must bow before him. How exquisite it would be to shatter that assumption.

Tomorrow, then.

Alaric found himself almost looking forward to it.

2

HAL

Hal's body throbbed with victory and pain as he ducked into his tent. Sweat had dried crusty beneath his armour, and every joint fought against him after the day's work. He'd felt it when his opponent fell—the shock running through his lance, up his arm, straight into his shoulder. That same shoulder now burned like fire. But pain was nothing next to winning. Pain was just what you paid for glory, and today, he'd earned his share and more.

"Perrin," he grunted. "Get this fucking metal off me."

"Yes, sir."

Perrin's hands were sure and swift, so Hal closed his eyes and let the young man work. The familiarity of it was soothing to him. The breastplate came away first, the dull gleam of the old metal further dimmed by the dust on the field. When he was freed from all that weight, he opened his eyes to watch his squire work. Perrin had the spatial awareness of a sheep safe in its herd, so Hal got to stare to his heart's content. He traced the lines of Perrin's face with his eyes—the soft curve of his jaw, the dark sweep of his lashes—framed by curls damp with sweat, his brow faintly furrowed in concentration. His skin, a deeper olive in the tent's shadows, bore a flush from exertion. The boy looked sweet as he bit his lower lip.

Ah, not a boy. Hal chided himself; he shouldn't think of Perrin that way. He was only two years younger than Hal, after all, a man at twenty-three. Technically too old to be a squire, but Perrin was too good to pass on. It was only that Perrin was short and soft around the middle, and couldn't grow any hair along his jaw, that Hal saw him as younger. There was softness in Perrin, elsewhere, too—in his eyes, most especially when those eyes lifted to meet Hal's own.

Hal felt a strange tightness in his chest as Perrin looked up at him, those large, expressive eyes holding something like admiration. It made Hal stand taller, made him want to puff out his chest and preen like some foolish cockerel. Perrin's gaze flicked away, and a red flush crept up the young man's neck, spreading to his cheeks. The sight of it sent a peculiar heat through Hal's own body.

And instead of saying anything he meant to, Hal blurted, "What's wrong with you, boy?"

Perrin's hands fumbled with the next buckle. "Nothing, ser," he murmured. Shit. He'd made his squire all sad again. Hal had a special way of doing that, it seemed. "Just thinking about the bout tomorrow."

Hal grunted, allowing Perrin to turn his attention back to the armour. When he was done, Perrin got to polishing, and Hal collapsed on the edge of his cot. His muscles were crying out to him, all of them making loud complaints about how many hours that week he'd been on the horse, how long he'd been in his armour, how long he'd had his damn arm outstretched holding the lance.

Pain was good, he tried to tell himself, but pain was also

loud, and harder to ignore at night. He decided he hated this part—after victory, after all the cheers—when his body reminded him it was just meat and bone. Even his skin betrayed him; he'd burned most of his neck out there. How he'd managed to be born with the pale skin of a sheltered noble, he couldn't guess, but it was surely the Gods' cruel joke. Hal sat there with his eyes closed, listening to Perrin scrub away. He tilted his head this way and that, stretching out the tightness in his neck. But in the silence, his victory cooled into stiffness, leaving him stranded. It was a triumph that meant little in the long run, and a pain he couldn't ignore for much longer.

This was a limbo only Perrin knew how to navigate.

"My shoulders," he said, watching Perrin rub his cuirass like his life depended on it. "They're fucking killing me."

Perrin's hands stilled on the breastplate he'd been cleaning. He set it down without a word—Hal never really had to *say* what he wanted, the squire could always guess—wiped his palms against his thighs and reached for the small clay pot of salve his lady patron had offered him at the last tournament. For the smell, she'd said; she'd wrinkled her nose at him when he tried to give her a favour from the lists. And she didn't want him sullying his surcoat, neither, since she'd paid a pretty penny for it. *Try to avoid the dust.* But that Hal couldn't do much about, not if he wanted to focus on a win.

He hadn't been using the salve—the perfume?—the way Lady Isolde Kerran had intended, but he was getting his use out of it. The clean, bright smell hit Hal the instant Perrin opened the jar. Pine and something sharper beneath, mint maybe. Perrin's fingers tested the consistency, warming it.

"You're taking too long," Hal said, though Perrin hadn't

been slow at all. He just enjoyed the way Perrin's whole body reacted to a light scolding; Perrin leapt to attention and sped over.

When his squire's hands finally pressed into the meat of his shoulders, Hal groaned, loud and shameless. This kind of contact used to make him flinch, the sudden intrusion of another person's heat against his skin. But Perrin was, in many ways, an extension of himself now, so the squire's touch felt expected. Wanted, even. It helped, Hal supposed, that Perrin knew what he was doing—the man's hands were probably the only strong thing about him.

The squire's thumbs dug into the knots where tension gathered, and Hal's breath hissed through his teeth.

"Too hard, sir?" Perrin asked, voice tight with concentration.

"Harder," Hal commanded, flashing a grin over his shoulder. "I'm not some delicate lordling who'll break. Put your back into it."

He wanted it to hurt before it helped. Wanted the pain to peak and break like a fever so he could sleep tonight without his body reminding him of all he'd demanded from it.

Perrin's touch altered, pressure increasing until Hal's eyes watered. Perfect. He leaned into it, making a show of his satisfaction. Let the boy know his worth. Not that Hal would admit needing anyone, but if he did — well, those hands were worth their weight in tournament gold.

"Fuck, that's good," he muttered, not caring how it sounded. "Keep that up, and I might just let you have tomorrow off."

Perrin suppressed a breathy laugh. "You don't mean that, sir."

"No," Hal chuckled, "I don't."

Hal breathed through Perrin's touch, focusing on the feeling of tissue yielding, the slow surrender of muscle that had been rigid all day. Eighteen months without defeat. Eighteen months of proving everyone wrong.

The thought swelled his chest with pride.

He remembered those first tournaments, how they'd laughed at his borrowed armour and common speech. But he'd shut them up, one by one, as lances splintered against shields and bodies tumbled into dust. The Upstart had a good first season, they'd conceded. The Upstart wouldn't last.

The Upstart was just lucky.

Well, luck didn't last eighteen fucking months. Skill did. Strength did. *Hal* did.

And now everyone said that title—which had been given to him as a mocking jab—with a little more respect. Ser Halden the Upstart was a knight worth remembering.

"Who'd I just beat?" Hal snorted, realising he'd already forgotten his last opponent's name and heraldry. They'd begun to blur together, all those polished young men with their expensive training and their shock when they found themselves unseated. "Had the fancy gold trim on the saddle."

"House Pidon. Third son." Perrin's fingers found another knot beneath Hal's skin. "Lord Merrin's nephew."

"Nephew to a lord and still rides with his elbow out like a tavern drunk." Hal laughed, the sound sharp with satisfaction. All that fancy training, and for what? "Like he'd never held a lance in his life. Practically asking to get knocked on his ass."

Perrin hummed in agreement, his hands moving now to the tightness in Hal's neck. "His balance was wrong from the start."

Hal slumped forward at Perrin's touch. Gods, this was bliss, even with all the angry muscle sending jabs of pain back into his skull. Almost too late, he realised Perrin had said something. . . Well, smart. "You noticed his balance."

It wasn't a question, but Perrin answered anyway. "I notice everything."

And he did. Maybe Perrin hadn't known the first thing about jousting when he'd started, but for two years now, he'd watched the circuit with those quiet eyes of his, and listened, and put things together in a way Hal could only dream of. His squire was bloody smart. He was the reason Hal had known which knights to challenge first in early tournaments with rolling lists, and which to avoid until he had more wins under his belt. More recently, Perrin was the one coming to Hal with all the gossip from other squires, so Hal knew who was injured and where, and who was a little unfit for the season and might easily fall off his horse three days into the competition. Perrin didn't just maintain Hal's equipment: he maintained his reputation, his strategy, his *edge*.

He was, in a way, the Upstart knight, too. But Hal would never tell him. Not on his life.

A sharp whistle at the tent's entrance made Perrin's hands jerk back from Hal's skin.

"Keep going," Hal ordered, catching Perrin's wrist before he could retreat completely. "My shoulders are still fucked."

Perrin hesitated—a sweet gasp of shock, a stiffening at Hal's fingers around his wrist—then resumed his work as Hal called out, "Enter."

The tent flap parted to reveal Lady Isolde Kerran, Hal's sponsor, and his good mood suffered a bit.

Here we bloody go.

His lady ducked inside, cheeks red from the walk and hands fussing as if she'd run the lists herself, her plain brown braid slipping loose over one shoulder. Her eyes were too bright, a strange blue that felt almost repellent to stare into, and they were set in a face that would never have turned a head if not for the name attached to it. Hal figured that was an alright thing to think, given he wasn't a pretty face himself. And Lady Isolde was, at best, very annoying to listen to.

She wrung her hands like being in his tent was all terribly thrilling and a servant—a thin, quiet fellow who probably had his ear talked off every hour of the day—worked to smooth the stretched seams of her wool riding dress, until she batted him away.

Hal tried to keep his expression tame. She was his lady, his patron, and even if she was odd as hell and turning up to tournaments without her husband like it was nothing, what could he do about it? Until he found someone better willing to back him, he was stuck with her and the piece of his future she owned.

"Ser Halden," she said, inclining her head in the barest acknowledgment. She gave an awkward grin and opened her hands. "Another victory."

"My lady." Hal didn't rise. Let her see him like this—bare-chested and unashamed, the knight she'd chosen to sponsor proving his worth. For whatever reason, one not even Perrin had come to guess, she was stuck with them, too.

Only in very specific ways could Hal use that to his advantage. Not moving right now was one of them.

Her eyes flickered to Perrin, whose hands continued their steady work on Hal's shoulders. A fraction of disapproval crossed her face, there and gone in a breath. Ha! He'd bet his life she wasn't used to this sort of treatment, no matter how small her noble house.

As if noticing Hal's semi-nakedness for the first time, Lady Isolde politely turned her gaze away. She addressed the tent flap, saying, "The crowd was particularly enthusiastic today." She snapped her fingers, and the servant produced a pouch. "Which makes for a healthy purse!"

The servant tottered forward and lowered the sack for Hal to take. Hal thought about snubbing it, just to see the look on his face. But shit, gold was gold. He snatched it from the servant's palm.

"House Pidon's pride will demand a wager on the next match," she continued. "I've encouraged their steward to consider it a matter of honour. So that's one for the next tournament to look forward to."

Of course, she had. Lady Isolde had a talent for making men feel they had something to prove. It had worked on Hal, once, and look where he'd ended up. Hal had been born indentured to House Fenholt and raised as one of many men-at-arms. For a long time, that made for an unremarkable life, until Lord Fenholt, whose holdings sat on the border between Valenne and Karsault, decided he wanted a little more land than he had. The Sevenfold Realm was a fucking big kingdom, but it still only took up a third of the supercontinent; Lord Fenholt was right in that there was plenty more land to be had, even if the way he went about it spelled inevitable war. Thus, Hal had been perfectly positioned to stop the lord's stupid son dying a stupid death, yanking the youth back in his saddle just in time to keep an enemy halberd from punching through his pale throat.

The act had earned Hal his knighthood, and things had been good for a time. Until Lady Isolde saw him trying to make a name for himself in the lists and approached.

"I hear rumours you saved Lord Fenholt's boy," she'd said.

"They are no rumours," Hal had replied.

Lady Isolde had only shrugged. "I hear rumours you made that story up. That you're some upstart who won't last the season." Hal had bristled at her words, and she'd put her hand out, like she meant for him to touch it. "I think you and I can prove them wrong."

So, sure, she'd manipulated his pride a bit. Still, she'd plucked him from obscurity with her patronage. But that debt had been paid in full with each victory and each coin he brought to her house's coffers. Not to mention the money she earned from her unscrupulous wagers, which—if that fat purse was anything to go by—earned a deal more than Hal's legitimate wins.

"Three more victories," she said, her voice taking on the edge of someone discussing a business transaction rather than feats of arms, "and we break the record for consecutive victories in the western circuit."

We. As if she'd lifted a lance even once in her life.

"There are three days left in this tournament before the season's over. If you aren't victorious, you'll have to wait for the next season to prove your worth." Next season was two months away, which wasn't a lifetime, but wasn't nothing when you lived off your winnings. Nor when the crowd's loyalties were fickle. "We don't want to wait that long, do we, hm?"

"I'm aware," Hal said. Perrin, the naughty thing, pressed a little harder on a sore spot, so Hal flinched and remembered his manners. "Thank you for your visit, my lady."

Lady Isolde smiled, hip popping to the side with glee. She clapped her hands together. "Oh, of course. Rest well, ser knight!"

She left without waiting for him to respond, simply turned and walked out with her servant. When the tent flap dropped closed, Hal took a deep breath. He wasn't usually so dramatic, but something about her presence fogged him up. With her gone, he could finally fill his lungs properly again.

He grabbed the money pouch she'd left, bouncing it in his hand. Heavier than before. That was good. But it didn't feel as good as it should've.

"She doesn't even like watching the jousts," he said to the empty air. "Just counts the coin they bring in."

Perrin's hands paused on his shoulders. "She secured your knighthood."

He rolled his eyes. "And reminds me of it at every turn."

Perrin, apparently, didn't know what to do with that. Anytime their conversations edged out of the familiar territory of his duties, the squire wavered. Now, his hands hovered awkwardly, and when he started up his movement again, an angry heat grew high in Hal's chest. He reached up and grabbed Perrin's wrist.

"Enough." Perrin's hands fell away. Hal waved the air next to him. "Sit down."

When the squire didn't move, Hal turned around. Perrin was hesitating, glancing at the equipment still in need of attention.

"I said sit."

The squire lowered himself to the edge of the cot, keeping a careful distance between them. Hal closed that distance with a shift of his weight and aligned their shoulders. Neither spoke. The sounds of the tournament grounds filtered through the canvas—distant laughter, the crackle of fires, the occasional whinny of horses settling for the night.

Without looking at him, Hal reached up and pressed Perrin's head down until it rested against his shoulder. The man stiffened for an instant, then softened, allowing his weight to settle against Hal's side. His hair smelled of the salve and of sweat. Of honest labour.

Hal let his own head tilt sideways until his cheek pressed against the crown of Perrin's head, the soft strands tickling his jaw. Perrin might have been just a squire, but a squire's duty was whatever his knight required. Right now, Hal required this.

The world narrowed to just that moment—to the warmth where they touched and the rhythm of their breathing gradually falling into sync.

Hal didn't acknowledge what he was doing, or why. Perrin had relaxed, so Hal could, too. He closed his eyes and breathed in the only comfort he would permit himself to need.

"You're facing the Nameless Knight."

Perrin, who could read much better than Hal, delivered this news very quietly. He'd run to the pairings board first thing and had returned to spout his findings. Hal was still in bed, and he'd stay in bed until the absolute last minute.

Perrin was looking at him like he expected anger.

But Hal only blinked at him. "Who the fuck is the Nameless Knight?"

He'd been on the circuit long enough to know every competitor worth knowing. Either this was some poor sod about to be humiliated, or. . .

Perrin shook his head. "I asked. He's some late entry. Only arrived yesterday."

That made Hal straighten. "But. . .I mean, he was allowed in? After registration closed?"

Perrin shrugged, a nervous motion. "I think," he began, then swallowed. "That is, ser, I know that schedules can be. . .flexible."

"For the right people," Hal finished with a scowl.

"Has to be a disgraced lord," Perrin said quietly. He was doing that thing he did when several overlapping thoughts came to him at once. A furrow appeared in his brow, and his eyes went far away. "Or someone's bastard with enough connections to matter. . .ser."

That last word was Perrin coming back to himself and his own anxiety, as if he'd said anything wrong by speculating about the undesirable past of his new competitor. Hal thought about Perrin's guesswork and frowned.

"You think he wanted to get slotted against me?" Hal snorted. What a fool. "Someone thinks highly of himself."

"Or someone paid very well to get the match they wanted."

Hal glanced at his squire. The boy was too observant for his own good sometimes. "You think he bribed his way in?"

Perrin's thin shoulders lifted in a half-shrug. "That scribe spent most of yesterday alone at his post. The marshal was in the stands. Also. . ."

Hal raised a brow. "Yes?"

"The scribe is wearing very fine boots this morning. From the merchant charging an arm and a leg for her leather work."

Hal's lips twitched, threatening a smile. "Ah." He threw back the covers and stood quickly, stretching his back until it popped satisfactorily. He was giving Perrin a view, he knew; he was amused by the way the squire's eyes kept glancing at his taut, barrel-sized chest and hairy belly, and, oh, lower still—Perrin was feeling quite bold that morning, apparently.

Hal reached for his clothes and began to dress. "So that's the first bracket?"

"The schedule was fixed," Perrin said, dogged as always when he sensed injustice on Hal's behalf. "You were to face Odenkirk first. An easy draw."

One of the three victories he needed to satisfy Lady Isolde. "And now this."

Going from a likely win to uncertainty stung.

Hal finished dressing and stepped into the weak sunlight, Perrin trailing behind. The tournament grounds were waking slowly, smoke rising from cook fires, voices calling across the trampled grass.

"He *must* have asked for you specifically, sir."

Hal stopped walking. A cold spike of something—not quite anger, not quite fear—drove through his chest. "You really think so?"

"Why else change the brackets? Any gap would have served if he just wanted to compete."

Hal resumed walking, faster now, his stride eating the distance to the lists where the day's matchups were posted. Around them, the encampment stirred with morning rituals: squires fetching water and running errands, knights emerging bleary-eyed from their tents. The smell of porridge hung in the air alongside wood smoke and horse dung.

The tournament herald had nailed the parchment to a post near the main pavilion. A small crowd gathered, murmuring over the changes. Hal shouldered his way forward, ignoring the glances that followed him.

It took him some time to read it, but there it was, right at the top.

First Bout: Ser Halden the Upstart vs The Nameless Knight

"Who is he?" Hal demanded of no one in particular, though heads turned at his voice. "Has anyone seen him ride?"

"Got a good horse, I heard," some anonymous voice declared behind him. "Thoroughbred."

Thoroughbred. Probably the Nameless Knight was just as well-bred, too. Hal turned and shoved back through the crowd.

"Show me," he commanded. Perrin was still trapped in the sea of bodies but ran out with purpose the moment he was free. The squire darted ahead and led the way through the sprawl of tents and pavilions to where competitors were allotted space according to their standing. The Nameless Knight's area was near the edge, and he only had a modest tent. A tent he didn't even own, by the patches on it. He'd hired the tent from the scribe.

But beside it was the famed mare, dozing in the early light. And that anonymous voice had been right; she was exceptional. Her coat was gleaming, her size and shape were perfect, and Hal knew this wasn't a beast you'd find in any common stable.

The armour laid out on a work cloth nearby was old and simple, but still had the shine of quality steel to it. Then the tent flap opened, and out the knight walked, and Hal's whole body seized up at the sight.

Hal had the unfamiliar sensation of being caught off guard. Hal's gaze raked over the stranger, jaw tightening with each detail. Tall, with the kind of lean muscle that suggested a natural build rather than Hal's own hard-won strength.

He wore his long black hair pulled severely away from a face too perfectly sculpted. High cheekbones pressed beneath sun-gilded skin; really, he seemed to glow beneath the morning rays. When the man glanced up, silver eyes catching the light, something twisted in Hal's gut. His breath shortened. His skin went hot beneath his tunic.

This didn't look like the sort of man who'd ever had calluses burst open mid-tilt. He looked too clean for this kind of life. For the reality of knighthood. Is that why Hal wanted so desperately to see that perfect face contorted in defeat?

Hal imagined the satisfaction of unseating him, watching that perfect body hit the dirt—then caught himself wondering how he'd look gripping a lance. How those large, strong hands might wrap around—

No. Hal looked away, then immediately back again.

The stranger smiled, and Hal's mouth went dry with the sudden, violent urge to wipe that expression away with his fist. Or his mouth.

"Fuck him," Hal muttered. "That's a lord, for sure."

And Hal couldn't be blamed for his attraction to a lord. There was something god-like about a noble's breeding. A proper noble, not like homely Lady Isolde.

But then the knight knelt beside his armour and began to tend it, methodically checking each strap and buckle.

"Doing his own work," Hal murmured, grudging respect colouring his voice.

"Or he can't keep a squire," Perrin suggested.

"With that horse?" Hal laughed. "He's rich."

"Of course, ser. But maybe he's a rich bastard."

Perrin was smiling softly when Hal looked over. He supposed the squire had a point—though he couldn't say *he* treated Perrin with the utmost respect. Hal was an indentured bastard, and he knew plenty of squires who'd prefer the lap of a rich bastard over his own. Most squires bore far more than Hal's loud frustration, though, and did it gladly. Surely, if this knight wanted help, he'd have it.

"Ser," Perrin ventured. He chewed on his words for a while. "Will he be trouble?"

Hal's mouth twisted. Damn it, Perrin. He fixed the boy, or rather, young man, with a look. "Never let me hear you doubt me again."

He turned away, mind already shifting to the bout ahead. He pictured the impact, the line of the charge, the precise angle needed to unseat a rider cleanly. His body understood these calculations better than his mind ever had. Numbers and letters had always danced before his eyes, but the language of force and motion—that he spoke fluently.

"Ser!" Perrin chased after him in a run. "I don't—I wasn't—!"

But Hal was thinking of Ser Pretty with that bright smile. "Eighteen months," he said as they walked back to their own tent. "Eighteen months since anyone's unhorsed me. He thinks he can beat me, Perrin, and it won't happen. I'm not letting some nameless bastard with a pretty horse and a pretty face end that streak."

"Of course not," Perrin agreed. "It's only, what if he's good? I mean, he asked for you specifically, and—"

"Then he's a fool." Hal's voice hardened. He stopped in front of the tent and turned to his wide-eyed squire. They still had an hour to prepare.

"One of the pauldrons needs adjusting after yesterday,"

he said. "Check my saddle for the balance. And check the lances. His, too, if you can manage; I don't want to be dealing with a nobleman's tricks."

Perrin nodded and ducked inside to complete the first of his tasks. Alone for a moment, Hal looked back across the camp in the direction of the Nameless Knight's tent.

The Upstart against the Nameless.

There would be no competition. Hal had earned his place here with blood and broken bones. No one—named or nameless—would take that from him.

3
ALARIC

Alaric fumbled with the last strap of his breastplate, fingers methodical—he knew what he was doing, of course—but stiff from a night on a plain pallet rather than silken sheets. He winced as leather chafed against sensitive skin unused to such rough quarters. Yet a small part of him savoured that discomfort. How quaint, to suffer like a common soldier.

Beyond the flap of his tent, dawn lay over the world in cold pewter light. Sleep had eluded him through most of the night—the thin mattress pricked at his noble-bred skin, yes, but more than that, his mind had refused to quiet. He'd been entranced with his bout against the Upstart, imagining every tilt of lance and angle of shield needed to bring the commoner-knight's winning streak to its inevitable end.

As if the outcome were ever in question.

But this commoner-knight forged by sheer ferocity and raw talent had drawn Alaric's curiosity sharper than any blade. He refused to wholly admit it, but he was intrigued by the Upstart's boldness, by the promise of meeting strength unfettered by titles or privilege.

Sliding on his plain helm, he smiled to himself: today, he was only the Nameless Knight, and that anonymity gleamed richly in his chest. The Upstart wanted to keep his win streak, no doubt. That would mean he wouldn't hold back. Perfect—Alaric did so hate an easy victory. But a victory it would be. The commoner's streak would end today, by his hand.

Fiona's soft nicker answered him as he stepped out, her breath steaming in the chill.

"Ready for this?" he murmured, running a gloved hand along her crest. The mare tossed her head with casual pride —of course she was ready. Bred and broken in since foal-hood, she was like him, in a way. That life of discipline would show him through today.

The tournament grounds had awoken overnight. Where yesterday the earth had seemed beaten down and weary, now tension crackled in the air. Trampled blades shimmered in silver, and the wooden barriers glistened under fresh gusts of wind that snapped pennons to attention. Every taut rope and polished stake spoke of promise—of violence and glory.

Of Alaric's assured win that morn.

Escorting Fiona toward the marshalling area, Alaric observed the rabble in their threadbare cloaks and mud-caked boots. These early-rising peasants pressed against each other like cattle, jostling for positions along the rails that his kind would never deign to touch. No velvet cushions here, no canopied boxes—just the stink of unwashed bodies and cheap ale. They came hungry for spectacle, and he felt a thrill meeting their eager eyes. If they knew a man of his station was masquerading in plain steel, the magic would vanish like morning mist. If he won, he would never know if it was his talent or his title that had granted him victory.

Let them all believe in the Nameless Knight.

"Ser," barked an attendant, beckoning him to the marshalling area. "First bout. Prepare yourself."

He checked his armour a final time; unmistakably fine in its fit and quality, yet deliberately unadorned. The man thrust Alaric's lance at him, noting with distaste how poorly balanced it was compared to the practice weapons Alaric had trained with at court. Compensating for its inferior craftsmanship, he tested it, feeling the flex of seasoned ash, the way it wanted to move in his grip. Alaric shifted until it felt like an extension of himself, the way all good fighters learn to use their weapons.

He ran a gloved hand down the lance's polished shaft, imagining the Upstart astride his own steed: muscular thighs, broad shoulders, the taut line of his jaw set with determined concentration. Then, those broad shoulders hitting dirt, that stubborn jaw slack with shock.

A flicker of something unspoken warmed Alaric's veins —anticipation, he decided. Excitement.

Everything was as it should be.

Then, across the lists, a ripple of movement caught his attention. A cry went out in the crowd, first bubbling up from the commoners who had gathered on his opponent's side, and then spilling forth into the grandstands. Here was the people's champion, the proof that any commoner could become great.

The Upstart had arrived.

Alaric watched him approach and, without meaning to, began to measure him.

The Upstart sat upon a broad-shouldered destrier, the

horse draped in his patron's yellow-and-blue. His armour was noticeably old, slightly out of fashion, but every dent and scratch had been coaxed into a muted gleam that did much to offset the agedness of the cuirass. Someone had cared enough to make it so.

That someone walked at Halden's stirrup.

The Upstart's squire, that skinny shadow Alaric had observed yesterday. Even now, the boy's attention never wavered from his knight, hands adjusting straps that needed no adjustment, checking fastenings already secure.

Alaric knew the look of duty well enough. But devotion, freely given? He had yet to experience that for himself. What Alaric and his title inspired was service. What stood before him now was something else entirely.

He shook his head clear; sentiment had no place in the lists. Besides, Alaric hadn't come here to find devotion. He wanted a victory that could truly be called his.

The Upstart turned, and for a moment their eyes met across the length of the lists. The impact was physical; Alaric's chest constricted in an odd way at the sight of the Upstart's aggressive confidence. The man was a brute, Alaric reminded himself, someone so far beneath Alaric's station that in any other context they wouldn't exchange words, much less lances.

And yet.

There was something in that line of the jaw, the breadth of the shoulders, something that made Alaric's pulse quicken in a way that had nothing to do with the approaching joust.

He looked away, annoyed at himself.

A groom appeared at Fiona's side, offering a mounting block Alaric didn't need. He swung into the saddle with practiced ease. Fiona shifted beneath him, her muscles tense with anticipation.

The squire—his temporary squire, borrowed from the tournament staff since he had none of his own—fumbled with the shield. It took three attempts to secure it properly to Alaric's arm, and by then his shoulder was already aching from holding it at the correct angle. No matter. Endurance was his strong suit.

"Visor, my lord?" the squire asked, then immediately flinched. "I mean—ser."

Alaric sighed; his bearing gave him away. But that didn't matter, either. Only this bout. "Yes. Lower it."

The world narrowed to a horizontal slit. The grandstand became a blur of colour and motion. The field compressed into a single line: the barrier running down its centre, and beyond it, Halden the Upstart.

Who was also lowering his visor now, his squire stepping back with visible reluctance. Alaric watched the way the young man's hand lingered on his knight's stirrup, the gesture both possessive and tender. Then Halden's heel touched his mount's flank, and the moment shattered.

A horn sounded, summoning both competitors to the centre of the field. Together they moved forward, meeting before the royal box, where a minor lord and his retinue served as the day's judges.

Up close, the Upstart was even more obviously a man who'd risen from struggle. His face bore the evidence of battles both in and out of the tournament—a nose that had been broken and reset more than once, a scar through one eyebrow that pulled his expression into a permanent challenge. His eyes were the bright green of a meadow, and they fixed on Alaric with immediate, instinctive hostility.

Alaric, for all his experience with catty nobility, shivered at that gaze.

"Ser Halden the Upstart," announced the herald, "victor of thirty-seven bouts, undefeated these eighteen months past, champion of the western circuit, knight of—"

"Get on with it," Halden muttered, just loud enough for Alaric to hear. Impatience radiated from him like heat from a forge. The herald spluttered a little but did as the Upstart wished. He gestured over to Alaric.

"—and his challenger, the Nameless Knight."

The silence that followed Alaric's non-introduction hung awkwardly in the air. The crowd stirred. A knight without lineage or achievement was an oddity, and the emptiness of his name against Halden's many wins felt nearly pathetic.

But after a lifetime of hearing his name dragged out into a litany of titles and expectation, to be underestimated was a gift.

The lord gave the signal, and both knights retired to their ends of the lists. The drums intensified. The crowd went tense; bodies pressed forward, and chatter simmered to low whispers. Everyone wanted to see if the Upstart's streak would continue, if today would be the day someone finally put him in the dirt.

The marshal raised his flag, and Alaric's world contracted to three things: the horse beneath him, the lance in his grip, and the distant figure of his opponent. Everything else—the crowd, the doubt, the mess of emotion—fell away like water off oiled leather.

The flag dropped.

Fiona surged forward, her powerful hindquarters driving them toward the barrier. Alaric couched his lance, feeling the weight distribute through his arm and shoulder. The distance between knights collapsed with each pounding hoofbeat. Through his visor, Halden grew from a distant figure to an onrushing threat, his own lance levelled with deadly precision.

Instinct guided Alaric. He had just enough time to mark the other knight's position—square in the saddle, lance arm steady, shield angled to deflect rather than absorb—before—

Impact.

Their lances struck shields simultaneously. The ringing crash was like a blacksmith's hammer on an anvil, the tolling of a bell.

The shock travelled up Alaric's arm, through his shoulder, into his spine. His lance had struck Halden's shield dead centre, but the Upstart's struck true as well. For a moment, they were locked together—two forces meeting with equal violence—and then they were past, slowing at opposite ends of the lists.

Alaric slowed Fiona to a canter, then a walk. He could feel his heart hammering against his ribs, taste copper at the back of his throat. His shoulder throbbed where the impact had driven armour into flesh. Real, he thought. This was real in a way court tournaments never were. No pulling punches, no false courtesy. Halden had meant to unhorse him.

Good.

Across the field, Halden had turned his mount and was walking back to his starting position. Even through the narrow slit of his visor, Alaric could read frustration in the set of those shoulders. The Upstart had expected to win on the first pass. Cocky bastard.

Eighteen months undefeated was about to become history.

The marshal's flag rose again.

Alaric adjusted his grip on the lance, feeling where the wood had splintered slightly from the first impact. He watched Halden settle into position, the subtle shift of weight that indicated readiness.

Then the flag dropped, and they were charging again.

This time, Alaric leaned fractionally forward, urging Fiona to an even faster charge. The mare responded instantly, her stride lengthening. The increased momentum would translate to greater impact force—a simple equation of mass and velocity that had decided tournaments since knights first lowered lances against one another. The ground disappeared beneath Fiona's hooves. Wind whistled through the slit in Alaric's visor.

Halden grew in his vision once more, but the knight's shield had shifted slightly higher. His lance tip wavered almost imperceptibly. Fatigue? Or anticipation of a different strike?

Alaric took a calculated risk and aimed just below the shield's centre, where the rim provided less protection. They converged, dust swirling around pounding hooves.

Alaric's lance struck the shield's upper edge with a crack that echoed across the field.

Both lance and rim shattered.

Halden's horse staggered, the impact driving the creature sideways. For a moment—one glorious, terrible moment—Alaric thought he'd done it. The Upstart swayed in his saddle, shield hanging useless, and the crowd gasped as one foot slipped from its stirrup.

But Halden kept his seat.

With remarkable athleticism, he hooked his leg back

into position and righted himself, finishing the pass upright if somewhat dishevelled. His lance had missed Alaric's shield entirely during the chaos of near dismounting.

The crowd erupted in chaotic noise, part disappointment, part appreciation for the display. Alaric circled back to his starting position, noting the change in Halden's demeanour. A thrill pulsed in him, but he had to stamp it down. *Stay focused.*

The Upstart's body language had shifted from confident to furious, tension visible in every line of his posture.

They slowed. Turned. Separated to opposite ends of the lists once more.

Alaric's breath came hard now, sawing in and out of his lungs. Sweat ran down his spine beneath the armour, pooling at the small of his back.

The borrowed squire handed him a fresh lance. This one balanced differently, heavier in the haft, and Alaric took a moment to adjust his grip. Across the field, Halden's squire was replacing his knight's ruined shield, the boy working with frantic efficiency. When he stepped back, Halden reached down and touched his shoulder, and the squire straightened as if that casual touch had been a benediction.

The field was churned mud where their horses had torn it apart. The crowd was placing final bets, shouting over the drums, and Alaric heard none of it. He had one more pass. One more chance.

The flag rose. In the endless space between heartbeats, Alaric thought of his father, who would skin him alive if he discovered his whereabouts. His mother, who had wanted a scholarly son over a warrior.

The courtiers who'd asked, with polite condescension,

why a man of his station would bother learning skills he'd never need to use.

Because, Alaric thought. *Because I wanted to know if I could.*

The flag dropped once more.

Alaric drove Fiona forward with everything they had left, lance levelled, aim unwavering. Halden charged to meet him.

Alaric made his decision in the final heartbeat before contact. Instead of aiming for the shield again, he shifted his target slightly to the left—where breastplate met shoulder. A difficult strike. But he could do it. He had to do it.

Their lances made contact simultaneously. Halden's struck Alaric's shield dead centre, but Alaric's found its mark at the junction of plate and articulated shoulder.

He felt the connection through every bone in his body; the lance shattering, Halden's armour buckling, the movement of mass. Halden's body twisted with the force, his centre of gravity shifting beyond recovery. He buckled, torso folding over the point of impact, and tilted to the side. A leg in the air, arms reaching for the reins—

And Halden left his saddle.

Alaric caught only a glimpse as he galloped past, but he spun in his saddle, eager to watch as Halden's heavy body collapsed under the strain of gravity. He plummeted, but at the last second, Halden managed to tuck his limbs. He fell in a controlled tumble, hitting the ground with a practiced roll. Dust erupted around him, briefly obscuring his landing.

Silence gripped the lists for a beat. Then two. Then the crowd exploded.

Alaric's hands trembled on the reins. His breath came in shudders. He'd done it. He'd beaten the Upstart. It was only in that moment that he recognised the undercurrent of emotion for what it was: relief. Had he truly doubted himself so enormously?

Alaric completed his pass and circled back to the fallen knight. Sweat plastered his hair to his forehead, and the chill air felt like a blessing against his overheated skin. He watched as Halden pushed himself to his feet, cursing as his squire tried to help him up.

The Upstart ripped open his visor, dust coating his reddened face. His eyes burned with something more complex than simple anger—humiliation, yes, but beneath it pulsed that deeper wound. Red-faced and angry, he reminded Alaric of an angry cat. Ser Halden was all fluffed up.

"Lucky shot," Halden spat, voice raw with emotion.

Alaric should have let it pass. Instead, he reached up and lifted his visor, just enough to expose his eyes. Adrenaline surged through him. Halden looked so furious, so adorable with his red-faced bravado, that Alaric couldn't help but smile. "Or maybe," he said, "your luck's finally run out."

The words hung between them as the wind picked up, snapping banners overhead like the crack of distant whips, muffling the crowd's cheers. Halden's expression cycled from surprise to anger, and in that moment, something passed between them.

Halden's squire tried again, offering support his knight didn't accept. "Ser—"

"I'm fine," Halden snapped, but his eyes never left Alaric's. "Who are you?"

"No one," Alaric lied.

"Eighteen months," Halden said, shaking his head in disbelief. "Eighteen months since anyone put me down."

A thrum of pride pulsed in Alaric's chest. "Yes. You were overdue."

Halden spat over his shoulder at that, fists balling at his sides. "Beginner's luck doesn't survive the season."

"Then I suppose, Ser Halden," Alaric said, lowering his helm back into place, "we'll see each other again."

4
HAL

Perrin's hand hovered near his elbow, and Hal shook it off so roughly that the squire flinched.

"Go back," he said. "Tend to the gear." His voice came out thin and weak, lacking the command he'd meant to project. Perrin opened his mouth to argue, saw something in Hal's face, and closed it again.

Good. At least one person today still knew when to back down.

The young man retreated across the churned field, glancing back twice before the crowd swallowed him. Hal watched until he was certain Perrin wouldn't return, then turned toward the far end of the grounds, where the Nameless Knight's modest tent stood apart from the rest.

His body catalogued its injuries with each step. Shoulder screaming where the lance had caught him. Hip throbbing from the impact with the ground. A dozen smaller hurts that would purple by nightfall. None of the physical aches touched the thing writhing in his chest; this hot, sick fury that had nowhere to go. Eighteen months. Eighteen fucking months of building something from nothing, of proving every sneering nobleman wrong, and it was gone. Shattered, and not just by anyone, but by some lordling playing at poverty.

Because that's what he was. Perrin was right, but in a way, Hal had known it the moment their eyes met across the field, had felt the truth of it in his bones the way he felt the balance of a lance or the tension in a horse's neck. The Nameless Knight carried himself with the unconscious arrogance of the nobility. He was snide, his accent educated, and not a lick of sportsmanship had been on his face when he'd peered down at Hal in the dirt.

He'd put Hal, a once-commoner, back in his place.

Maybe your luck's finally run out.

The loss itself he could survive. But the way the bastard had said *that*, as if every win under Hal's belt had been chance. . .! As if skill and discipline and endless, grinding work meant nothing next to the poise and grace of a noble's lifelong training.

Fuck. That.

When he reached the tent, the flap was closed, and no one tended to anything outside. The quality mare dozed at her picket, coat gleaming despite the morning's exertion. Hal stared at her, wondering how much she cost. More than all his wins combined? More than himself? She was better bred than him for sure.

Hal breathed heavily and then did something rather stupid: he shoved through the tent flap without announcing himself and stepped inside.

The Nameless Knight stood at the tent's centre, half-stripped of his armour. His chest was bare beneath the gambeson he was peeling away, the linen shirt beneath it soaked with sweat. His dark hair hung loose around his face, freed from whatever tie had held it during the joust. In the dim light filtering through canvas, his skin gleamed with exertion, and Hal's eyes traced the lean muscle of his shoulders before he could stop himself.

He turned to look at Hal and didn't startle. The same calm he'd had on the field embraced him now, and he fixed Hal with a slightly raised brow. Hal, still in his hulking armour, felt suddenly very stupid. The Nameless Knight was acting like furious men burst into his tent every day.

Perhaps they did. Perhaps this was just another game to him.

"Ser Halden," the knight said. His voice was measured, cultured, precisely designed to piss Hal right off. "Can I help you?"

"What the fuck was that?"

The question came out rough with anger. Hal stepped forward, letting the tent flap fall closed behind him. The space was modest but well-appointed—a proper cot rather than a straw pallet, leather saddlebags.

The knight's smile froze. It was still polite, but taut, now, with anger. Hal guessed no one ever spoke to him this way. "Excuse me?"

"Who are you? Huh?"

"I told you," the knight said, turning back to his armour. His hands moved over the fastenings with familiar ease. "No one."

"Bullshit."

Hal crossed the remaining distance between them in three strides. His hand closed on the knight's bare shoulder and spun him around. The contact sent something jolting through his palm—heat, solidity, the shocking intimacy of skin against skin. The knight's eyes widened for just a moment, silver-grey and startled, before that infuriating calm reasserted itself.

"You bought your way onto the lists," Hal said, not releasing his grip. "Paid that clerk to slot you against me specifically. I know you did."

"And if I did?"

"Then you're pathetic." The word tasted good, *felt* good, a small reclamation of power. "Some lord's son slumming it for thrills. Playing at being an unsponsored knight because your real-life bores you. You have no idea what it actually means to earn something, so you had to take it from *me.*"

The knight's jaw tightened, the smile slipped, and oh, finally! Hal had broken through that hardened exterior. Yeah, there was a man in that cold shell like any other. Hal felt a surge of vicious satisfaction and pressed his advantage, stepping closer until their bodies were nearly touching, until he could smell the sweat and leather and something else beneath, something clean and expensive that had no business existing in a tournament tent.

Hal's voice dropped low. "One victory means nothing."

The knight relaxed. "Is that so? Then why are you having a tantrum in my tent?"

Hal's hand tightened on his shoulder. The knight's skin was warm beneath his palm, damp with cooling sweat. Hal was close enough to see the pulse beating at the base of that aristocratic throat, to count the individual lashes framing those maddening eyes.

Words got to him too easily. It was a flaw of his, his father had always said so, and Hal had proved that flaw over and over again. Not this time. His body thrummed with the urge for violence, but he made himself speak the anger aloud. "You think you can throw around enough coin to buy a shortcut, and suddenly you're a champion? You're nothing. You're worse than nothing—you're a fraud."

The knight's brow furrowed. "Are you sure about that?"

He looked Hal up and down, stare withering. "What exactly bothers you the most? That I paid for the opportunity to challenge you, or that I beat you? Quite easily, I might add."

Hal bit down on his tongue. He was gripping the knight so firmly; he was sure his nails were digging into the man's pale skin.

"You got lucky," Hal snarled.

A dazzling, pitying smile. "We both know that's not true."

The words hit him harder than his fall from the destrier.

Hal felt them settle in his chest, heavy and unwelcome, because he knew—before pride rushed in to protest—that they were true. There had been nothing lucky about that last pass. He could see it now, replay it in the space behind his eyes, the clean line and the perfect timing, and he knew: only skill could have landed that shot.

But the recognition still twisted in him. That kind of precision didn't come from stolen hours or hard-won bruises. It was forged the way noble skills always were: slowly, a masterwork weapon started in childhood, shaped under the guidance of proper tutors, refined with good gear and endless time, until instinct became second nature.

It wasn't something an upstart could ever compete with. Hal knew he should leave the tent and let Perrin massage out all the anger, but he just couldn't let it go. Turning around now felt like another, worse defeat. Hal had lost his streak today, but this lying, cowering noble's son could lose something too. If Hal could just push him hard enough.

"Tell me who you are," Hal demanded. His voice had gone hoarse. "Tell me what fucking house spawned you, what title you're hiding from. I want to know whose son just ended my streak."

"Does it matter?" The knight studied him, and Hal had the uncomfortable sensation of being read like a book. After he made some assessment, the Nameless Knight tilted his head and brought his strong arms to cross under his chest. His arms formed a kind of shelf for his firm pectorals, but Hal wasn't looking at that. "You want to know who I am to save what's left of your pride. If I outrank you sufficiently, you can tell yourself you never stood a chance. That the game was rigged from the start."

Hal bristled. "It is rigged."

"Yes." The admission surprised Hal. Something softened in the knight's expression, but it was a look that skirted too close to pity for Hal to like it.

"But *I'm* not rigging it against *you,* Ser Hal. I came here to test myself, nothing more."

"Against me specifically."

"Against the best. By every measure, that was you."

It should have been a compliment; it was probably intended as a compliment. Instead, it twisted in Hal's gut, and he couldn't—wouldn't—allow himself to accept it. Eighteen months had to mean something. He was still gripping the knight's shoulder, still standing close enough to feel the heat radiating from that lean body. His own breathing had gone shallow.

"You think flattery will make me forget you humiliated me in front of the entire fucking circuit?"

"No," the Nameless Knight said, voice softening to a silken drawl. The knight's lips curved, but his eyes hardened. "I think you've been jousting against washed-up has-beens and green noble boys playing at knighthood. Your undefeated streak?" He gave a dismissive flick of his fingers. "A commoner beating the dregs no real knight bothers with. Today was simply. . .a correction."

Something snapped in Hal's chest. He raised his fist without deciding to, muscle memory taking over, the same instinct that had carried him through countless brawls before he ever touched a lance. He was going to hit this smug, beautiful, insufferable bastard. He was going to wipe that knowing smile off his face and make him bleed, make him hurt, make him feel even a fraction of the humiliation burning in Hal's gut—

The knight's hand closed around his wrist.

The grip was firm but not painful, the fingers long and surprisingly strong. Hal's fist hovered between them, arrested mid-swing, and he found he couldn't pull free.

Perhaps it was only shock keeping him there. The knight's eyes held his, silver-grey and suddenly very close, and Hal realised with a lurch of something like panic that their faces were inches apart.

He could see the texture of the knight's lips. Slightly parted. Slightly dry. Hal had the insane urge to wet them with his own.

The knight smiled.

This smile was worse than the knight's cruel words. It seemed to gloat with understanding. It saw something in Hal he wanted no one to see. It reached into Hal's chest and found all the tangled, contradictory impulses he'd been ignoring—the anger that wasn't just anger, the way his body had responded to this proximity.

"Interesting," the knight murmured. His breath ghosted across Hal's lips.

That broke the spell. Hal wrenched his arm free with a violence that sent him stumbling backward, his heel catching on the edge of the knight's cot. His body betrayed him—pulse thundering in his throat, stomach twisting, skin prickling with heat that started at his neck and blazed upward. His hands wanted to shake. His lungs couldn't get enough air. The knight was watching him calmly, so relaxed that Hal knew the Nameless Knight would let him approach him, let him. . .

Every instinct screamed to either flee or surge forward, and he couldn't tell which urge terrified him more.

"Stay away from me," he snarled. This was a trick, something to get in his head. And by the Gods, was it working.

The knight remained where Hal had left him, hand still extended as if holding a phantom fist. That smile lingered at the corners of his mouth, infuriating and knowing and entirely too pleased with itself.

"We're both on the tournament circuit, Ser Hal. Our paths will cross again."

There were only two days left to this tournament, but the knight had all but confirmed he'd be at the next, two months from now.

"Then I'll beat you next time. Properly. On the field."

"I look forward to it."

Hal didn't answer. But as he turned, the knight offered something of a peace offering.

"Alaric," he said.

Hal turned back to stare at him. "What?"

The man shrugged. "A not so Nameless Knight now."

Hal's nostrils flared; why had that made him more furious? He turned and shoved through the tent flap, emerging into late morning light that nearly blinded him after the dim interior.

The tournament grounds sprawled before him, unchanged by his world's quiet collapse. Squires ran errands. Horses were being exercised. The next competitors were taking their positions at the lists, their drama unfolding independent of his. No one looked at him. No one knew what had just happened in that tent—the almost-punch, the almost-kiss. He ground his teeth.

He was Ser Halden the Upstart, a year and a half undefeated until this morning, a knight who had clawed his way up from nothing through discipline and determination. He didn't have room for complications. Didn't have room for silver-grey eyes and knowing smiles and whatever the hell had just happened.

The crowd swirled around him, oblivious to his turmoil, and he walked aimlessly until he was at the edge of the grounds where the merchant stalls gave way to open field. A wooden fence marked the boundary, weather-beaten and listing slightly. Hal gripped the top rail with both hands and stared out at nothing in particular.

His knuckles were white. His breathing was ragged.

He thought about the knight's hand on his wrist. The precise pressure of those fingers. His lips.

Alaric's lips.

No. The Nameless Knight—he needed to stay the Nameless Knight—was a distraction at best. An enemy in truth. He'd taken Hal's streak, his pride, and would doubtless come for more if given the chance. He was not beautiful. He was not intriguing. He was not worth thinking about at all.

He was worth beating, though, and that was the task to which Hal would dedicate himself. He'd reclaim his pride with his next bout the following morning. He would win his final on the tournament's last day, and by the time they met again in two months, Hal's singular fall from grace would be long forgotten.

Behind him, somewhere in that modest tent, the Nameless Knight was probably still smiling.

5
PERRIN

Perrin did not go back to the tent.

He meant to. He made it a good twelve paces toward the yellow-and-blue canvas, and then his feet betrayed him. His duty was clear—prepare the tent, ready the evening meal, wait for Hal to return so he could polish the dented armour—but then he stopped near a merchant's stall and turned. His eyes tracked Hal's path across the churned earth of the tournament grounds.

The violence of being shaken off still hummed in his arm. Hal's hand had been rough, the dismissal absolute, and Perrin had obeyed the way he always obeyed. Years of service had taught him first to weather Hal's strange moods, but also to read the moments when any argument was futile. This had been one of them. Hal's face had been a door slammed shut, the fury behind it near audible.

Something stronger than duty held him in place now: The memory of Hal's face when the Nameless Knight had unseated him, his shock giving way to humiliation, then that dangerous anger that always made Perrin's chest tighten. Hal liked him for his obedience, but Perrin couldn't stop wondering what it was about this stranger that had gotten under Hal's skin so quickly. Was it just the defeat? Or something. . . else?

The merchant's stall sold leather goods. Anyone glancing his way would see a squire at loose ends, killing time while his knight handled other business, but Perrin was fairly unremarkable; even on his best days, few people noticed him. Even the merchant herself hadn't noticed him, busy as she was stamping a design into a purse. So now, Perrin positioned himself against the back support post, angling his body in a way to suggest he was examining the display and not watching helplessly as his knight's broad shoulders disappeared into the Nameless Knight's tent.

Everything continued. The tournament grounds hummed with activity around him, and no one else cared that Hal the Upstart had just stormed into the Nameless Knight's tent, because what did it matter, in the end? What were a few terse words between knights, if a tad uncouth? Why did this feel like the end of Perrin's world?

Perrin pressed his back against the post and tried to steady his breathing. His hands found the edge of a bridle, and he gripped it without purpose, the leather warm from the morning sun. He needed something to hold. Needed to feel solid in his body while his mind spun through possibilities he couldn't see or control.

What if Hal hit him? What if the Nameless Knight hit back? Perrin's free hand curled against his thighs, fingers pressing into the worn fabric of his breeches. He should go. Should intervene, should pull Hal away before he did something that would cost them everything—their place on the circuit, Lady Kerran's patronage, the carefully constructed life they'd built together.

Only, the more he imagined what was happening in the tent—Hal's fist connecting with that aristocratic jaw, the sound it would make, the satisfaction it might bring, Hal emerging with bloodied knuckles and a grim smile, the balance restored through simple violence—the less it felt right. It wasn't realistic.

Hal had been as trampled by nobility as anyone born a commoner. Would it really only take eighteen months in the lists collecting victories as a knight to erase his tolerance for highborn smugness?

Well, Perrin couldn't be sure about that. Hal wasn't the most chivalrous of knights, and his pride was an easily wounded thing. Perrin kept trying to tell himself it made sense for Hal to be so put out. Yet, he couldn't shake the unnameable feeling pressing at the edges of his awareness like a brewing headache.

Because, well, the Nameless Knight was beautiful.

Perrin thought about the knight. Had been thinking about him since that morning, if he was honest with himself, since the man had stepped out of his tent. Perrin had watched the joust this morning with the professional attention of a squire evaluating technique, but beneath that calculation, something else had stirred.

Perrin could name it plainly in himself, because truth was better than lying, he'd always been taught. The Nameless Knight, with his dark hair, and sharp face, and graceful movement, was beautiful. His body was lean, where Hal's was broad, built for speed rather than impact. There had been something almost elegant in the way he'd taken his victory, and maybe Hal had noticed that, too.

And now Hal was in that tent with him, and the noticing had turned into something sharp and uncomfortable in Perrin's chest.

It made sense. He told himself this as the seconds dragged on, as the tent flap remained closed and still. It made sense that two men like that would see something in each other. They were matched in a way that went beyond the tournament brackets—both young, both skilled, both possessed of that particular intensity that set them apart from the dozen other competitors who would ride and fall and be forgotten. Hal with his rough edges and hard-won glory. The Nameless Knight with his mystery and his cultivated anonymity.

They would look at each other and see a mirror, distorted but recognisable.

Perrin saw it, too. Which was part of the problem, wasn't it?

He thought about Hal's face in the morning light, still soft from sleep before the day hardened him. The reddish gold of his hair when it caught the sun. The crooked nose that should have been ugly, but somehow anchored his features into something compelling. The breadth of his shoulders, the way his body filled space, the way Hal trusted Perrin to knead out the pain in his shoulders. Perrin had spent years mapping that body; every scar, every tension, every place where the armour needed adjustment to accommodate old injuries that still pulled when the weather turned cold.

He knew Hal. Knew him the way a squire knew his knight, which was to say intimately and impersonally at once. He knew the sounds Hal made in his sleep. The way his appetite shifted before a bout. The exact set of his jaw when he was angry versus when he was afraid, and how rarely anyone else could tell the difference.

What he didn't know—what he'd been avoiding

knowing—was what to call the thing that tightened in his chest when Hal's hand fell on his shoulder. The warmth that spread through him when Hal said his name. The way his eyes tracked Hal's movements even when there was no tactical reason to watch, when the watching was just. . . wanting.

You're possessive, Perrin realised suddenly, and with great shame. Possessive of Hal, the way a dog might be possessive of its master; fierce and loyal and ultimately absurd with the extent of his feeling.

Hal barely knew he existed beyond the function he served. Perrin was the hands that managed the armour, the voice that reported on competitors, the shadow that anticipated needs before they were spoken. He was useful. Valued, perhaps, in the way one valued a good tool.

But he was not seen. Not the way he wanted to be seen, not the way Hal had seen the Nameless Knight—or the Nameless Knight had seen him.

And now Hal was in a tent with a beautiful stranger, and Perrin was standing outside with his hands on a bridle he had no intention of buying, and the jealousy was so sharp he could taste it like blood at the back of his throat.

The tent flap moved.

Perrin's breath stopped. His fingers tightened on the leather until his knuckles ached.

Hal emerged into the morning light. The expression on his face was—different. Gone was the defeated fury he'd entered with, though the loss still clearly weighed on him. Neither was he triumphant, though something had happened inside that tent. His expression was tense and nervous, a kind of disturbance that went deeper than anger, deeper than humiliation.

He looked like. . .he'd understood something suddenly, and now didn't know what to do with the knowledge. Or perhaps Perrin was seeing himself in that expression (for what was he to do about his feelings)?

Nothing at all, you fool.

Perrin tracked his knight's movements across the grounds, noting he stalked not back toward their tent, but aimlessly. Hal held himself rigidly, appeared to walk with purpose, but his eyes were far away, and he walked without destination.

Perrin almost went to him, the instinct running bone deep. Hal was in distress; therefore, Perrin should offer comfort. Wasn't that his very purpose?

But Hal had shaken him off, had made the line between them clear, and Perrin had to remember he wasn't anything but Ser Halden the Upstart's squire.

Perrin stayed where he was, half-hidden behind the merchant's stall, and let himself feel all of it. The attraction —yes, to both of them, the knight with his sharp beauty and Hal with his blunt presence. The resentment—toward the Nameless Knight for winning, and ultimately for drawing Hal's attention in a way that Perrin never had. Toward Hal himself, for not seeing, *for never seeing*, and for treating Perrin as furniture while chasing after a stranger who had humiliated him in front of everyone.

It was a tangled thing in his chest, the wanting and the anger, and Perrin put his head in his hands. These feelings weren't compatible with his life and his duty. Perrin had to put them aside.

He looked up.

Across the grounds, Hal had reached the fence at the edge of the tournament grounds, his white-knuckled hands gripping the rail as he stared at nothing.

The Nameless Knight's tent remained still.

There was work to be done. Perrin was a squire, and his knight had another bout before the afternoon.

Perrin put aside all his emotions and walked back to the tent.

6

ALARIC

The following morning, on the penultimate day of the tournament, Alaric's opponent fell with disappointing ease. Pathetic. Alaric's lance had struck with precision while the other knight's had wobbled uselessly, the impact nothing more than a mosquito bite against Alaric's shoulder. Nothing like the delicious shock of facing the Upstart. Even with the win, Alaric had earned nothing like the bone-deep satisfaction he'd felt unseating Halden.

The peasants cheered, but not loudly enough. They wanted blood and drama, not the efficient execution he'd delivered. Alaric couldn't fault them. He'd proven he could win without his title, but where was the glory in crushing insects?

Only Halden had made his pulse quicken. Only Halden had forced him to actually try.

Alaric tossed Fiona's reins to a waiting groom and strode from the field, already bored with today's victory and fixated on tomorrow's challenge. The tournament crown was practically his already—he'd outscored every opponent despite his late entry. He should have been savouring his inevitable triumph, but the thought tasted stale. Meaningless.

He needed Halden.

The scribe was still hunched over his ledgers like a gargoyle when Alaric entered the registration pavilion. No need for pleasantries this time. Alaric extracted a leather pouch from his boot and dropped it onto the desk with a satisfying clink of silver, heavy enough to snap the man to attention.

"You again," the scribe muttered, eyes widening at the purse. "Ser Nameless Knight. Your performance is most impressive."

"Tomorrow's brackets," Alaric said, cutting to the point. "I want them changed."

The scribe blinked. "The brackets are set, ser. Final matches arranged."

"And schedules are flexible, as we have well learned." Alaric smiled the smile that had so often opened doors and legs across the kingdom. "I want Halden again."

"The Upstart? He's matched with Ser Duncan of House Marlowe. A worthy challenger."

Not worthy of licking my boots, Alaric thought.

"I'm certain he is," he said smoothly. "But I defeated Halden through mere fortune, or so he claimed. I'd like the opportunity to prove his. . .mistake."

In the end it had been almost laughably simple, and Alaric found himself anticipating tomorrow not with the hollow certainty of another easy victory, but the sharp edge of genuine challenge.

He turned from the pavilion to find Ser Halden's next bout already underway.

Even across the field, Alaric's blood quickened at the

sight of him. Halden's mount pawed the earth, sensing its rider's fury. The man's easy confidence had burned away, leaving something dangerous in its place—a man, now, with everything to lose. Oh, how Alaric's win had upset him. Halden's shoulders coiled with the tension of a drawn bow. But the Upstart's opponent—some northern lord—was already defeated before the signal, Alaric could see it plain.

They crashed together with a force that silenced the crowd. Lances exploded into splinters and both riders rocked in their saddles. But only Halden commanded his seat through sheer will. The northern lord slammed into the packed earth with a sickening crack of armour and bone, and Halden thundered past without acknowledgement.

The crowd's roar hit like a physical wave. Their Upstart had returned, their champion restored. But even as Alaric nodded at Ser Halden's brutal display, he alone saw the truth beneath the triumph—the white-knuckled grip as Halden tore off his helm, the barely contained tremor that wasn't exhaustion but rage. Or. . .fear.

He was reliving their encounter yesterday. Alaric would bet his life on it. Halden the Upstart had attacked this poor, unsuspecting knight with all the anger he held for Alaric, and not even a victory was enough to quell the storm in him.

So Halden was the same as him, or similar; utterly unable to back down from a challenge. Heat surged through Alaric's veins, a hunger sharper than any desire for tournament glory.

Alaric watched Halden swing from the saddle, iron eyes fixed on the ground, while a scrawny squire darted forward as though Halden had split the very earth for him. The boy's devotion was exquisite torture to witness—raw, unguarded loyalty poured endlessly into a vessel too consumed by inner demons to recognise its worth. Did Halden feel those dark eyes burning into him? Did he understand the power he held over that desperate heart?

Never. Men like Halden, who clawed their way up through blood and grit, were blind to treasures freely offered at their feet.

But he sees you, a terrible voice urged in Alaric's ear. *You share the same demons; he is your brother-in-arms.*

Alaric shook his head. Not quite. Halden was raw talent to Alaric's precision. He was loud, potty-mouthed, and aggressive, which were traits Alaric had rarely encountered in his life. It was the heart of him, buried at his core, that Alaric recognised. That Alaric wanted to know.

In a way, though, the best way to know Halden the Upstart was to put him in the dirt again. Who would rise up from the ground that time, Alaric wondered? What kind of man would he become after a second humiliating defeat?

Only one way to find out.

The afternoon stretched ahead, empty and unsatisfying. He could return to his tent, could rest and prepare for tomorrow's final match. But restlessness clawed at him, the particular frustration of energy with nowhere productive to go.

The training grounds lay at the eastern edge of the tournament complex, a broad field marked with practice posts and weapon racks and then the rest of the field was given over to quintain, a post with a shield and counterweight for practicing ducking whilst on horseback. Most knights avoided the training grounds during competition days, preferring to conserve their strength, but Alaric had always found inactivity more draining than effort. His muscles craved work, demanded the satisfaction of genuine exertion.

He retrieved his practice sword from his tent—a plain, well-balanced bit of steel—and made his way through the afternoon heat to the grounds. Footprints marked the dirt, wooden posts bore fresh gashes, and the air carried the unmistakable tang of exertion. The practice posts stood in neat rows, each carved to roughly human proportions. Alaric selected one and began his routine—thrust, parry, riposte, the eternal dance of blade against imagined opponent. His shoulder muscles, tight from the morning's lance work, slowly loosened as he found his rhythm.

The sword sang through air, a silver arc of controlled violence. Alaric's muscles burned with each strike, sweat already darkening his shirt as he drove the blade into imaginary flesh and bone. Somewhere about the quarter-hour mark, it stopped being practice and became exorcism—each thrust purged the convoluted feelings from his body.

His breath came harder, faster, as he imagined real opponents falling before him instead of empty air, as he imagined someone in particular, broad shouldered and

Gravel crunched behind him. Alaric finished his sequence with a savage overhead cut that would have cleaved a man from crown to collarbone, then pivoted, blade still raised.

Halden stood at the edge of the field, knuckles white around a practice sword of his own. A muscle jumped in his jaw, and those green eyes—the same that had locked with Alaric's yesterday in his tent—burned with barely contained fury. The victory that should have restored his pride truly had done nothing to cool his blood.

"Nameless Knight." Halden's nostrils flared; he looked like a child resenting having to share his favourite toy.

Alaric bowed with a deliberate flourish, watching how Halden's throat tightened at the gesture. "It's Ser Alaric, Ser Halden. Your performance earlier was. . .quite adequate."

Halden advanced, tension radiating from his shoulders. "Adequate? Fuck off. I know you've bought your way into facing me tomorrow."

The accusation hung between them, but Alaric couldn't help but smile. This only made Halden's expression tighter.

"I'm merely a persuasive person," Alaric murmured. "I want to see you on your back again."

Halden spat over his shoulder, but a flush had assaulted his face. "Burn, you bastard."

Halden stalked to a practice post nearby, close enough that Alaric could smell the leather and sweat on him. His first strike hit with such force that splinters flew from the wooden target. The second strike came harder still, his grunt of effort carrying across the field like a battle cry. It was, for all intents and purposes, another tantrum.

So why did Alaric find himself watching Halden the Upstart for far too long?

Alaric pulled himself back to his own practice and matched Halden's rhythm stroke for stroke.

Steel bit into wood with violence and vicious precision —Halden's blade hacking chunks from his target, while Alaric's carved more precisely. Sweat drowned their tunics, salt stung eyes and slicked palms against sword hilts. The rhythm of their parallel training created a war-drum cadence across the field.

For twenty minutes they worked without words, but Alaric felt Halden's attention burning against his skin. Those green eyes would flick toward him between strikes, lingering longer each time, the same dangerous awareness that had sparked between them yesterday.

Halden suddenly drove his blade deep into the practice post with a crack that echoed across the field. He wrenched it free and turned, chest heaving.

"Enough of this horseshit," he spat, gesturing at the mutilated post with his blade. "I'm not getting what I need from dead wood."

What kind of wood...

Alaric did not finish that thought. He planted his sword point in the dirt, leaning on the pommel with practiced nonchalance. "And what exactly do you need, Ser Halden?"

"You." Halden levelled his practice sword at Alaric's chest. Alaric jolted—did Halden know how he teased? Was he deaf to his own insinuations? —but Halden followed with, "Fight me. Now."

The raw command hung between them, and Alaric's mouth curved into a slow smile as heat spread through his chest.

"Careful what you ask for. I've already beaten you once, and you're getting unhorsed again tomorrow."

Halden's jaw tightened, a muscle jumping beneath sweat-slicked skin. "Dammit, man. Draw your sword."

Alaric acquiesced, pulling his blade free from the ground. They squared off across churned earth, blades raised. This close, Alaric could count the speed of the pulse hammering in Halden's throat, could see the scar cutting through his left eyebrow, could measure the breadth of shoulders built for power rather than speed.

Brutish. Dangerous. *Perfect.*

Halden lunged first, a brutal thrust that slammed into Alaric's blade with a deafening clash. His plain steel screamed under raw force, foot sliding back with Halden's weight. Alaric barely pivoted his wrist, realigning his body so the blow skidded away harmlessly, but Halden's follow-up came like a hammer. A brutal slash that rocked Alaric backward as he barely raised his blade in time, then another aimed for his forearm that had him conceding too much ground. The Upstart lacked the finesse Alaric was used to in duels; he was raging ferocity, and every impact sent shockwaves pulsing up Alaric's arm, numbing bone and muscle alike.

But Alaric was a strategist. He let the next furious cut past his guard, luring Halden close, then delivered a lightning riposte aimed at his ribs. The blade whistled through the air, inches from flesh, and Halden had to jerk sideways to avoid it. The momentum carried them so close together that Alaric could taste the salt of Halden's sweat on his tongue. The tang of fear and fire filled his nostrils.

They backed up and circled each other like predators. Halden's brute strength thundered through every parry, every savage strike that sparked off Alaric's guard. Yet raw power, Alaric knew, was never enough, and Halden was becoming more and more predictable. Alaric began to track the hesitation before Halden's cuts, the minuscule lean of his weight before a thrust.

In a heartbeat, Alaric shifted from defence to assault. A feinted thrust to the shoulder, pulled at the last second to send a jolt of panic through his opponent. A wicked arc that would have maimed Halden's sword arm if Halden hadn't buckled in a messy dip to avoid it. Fury flickered in Halden's green eyes, gold flecks sparkling, his breathing ragged. His attacks grew wild and reckless.

Then Alaric overreached.

He'd been baiting for the perfect opening, a decisive thrust to end the duel, when Halden shattered every expectation. Instead of dodging, Halden lunged forward, body meeting blade with calculated abandon. Their swords locked at the cross guards, weapons clattered to silence, and suddenly they were chest to chest. Alaric panted. Halden's own ragged breath curled hotly over his face. Every one of their muscles was trembling.

Up close, Alaric felt the tremor of Halden's strength pressing back, and felt the dark heat pulsing from their bodies as their breaths synchronised into a single, frantic rhythm. In that suspended heartbeat, Alaric's pulse thundered in his ears; he couldn't tear his gaze from Halden's mouth. Imagined, foolishly, tasting it.

Training snapped him back into focus. No. No, he wouldn't do that. If Halden wanted brute power over finesse and grace, let him have it. He shifted one foot as if to yield, then dropped low with a savage sweep. His iron-shod boot struck sinew—an outlaw's manoeuvre outside any honourable school of swordcraft.

Halden howled in shock as his legs collapsed beneath him. His sword flew from his grip in a metallic arc. He crashed to the ground, breath rasping, eyes wide with shock.

"Bastard move," he grunted.

Alaric straightened, blade lowered, the dirty victory thrumming through his veins like wildfire. Gods, he would have been scolded hard for a move like that in court. But here? Well, the duel was over. "I'll see you in the morn," he said, turning away.

But he'd underestimated Halden's resilience.

Something happened in Alaric's periphery. By the time he'd turned, Halden had rolled, grabbed a shield from one of the practice dummies, and launched himself back to his feet. Before Alaric could react, Halden was charging shield-first.

The impact slammed the air from Alaric's lungs.

Halden's weight crashed down, the shield's iron rim biting just below his sternum and knocking all the air from his lungs. They collapsed in a writhing tangle of limbs and curses. Alaric's sword skittered free across the churned earth as they rolled, each man desperate to seize dominance.

Halden was a mountain of muscle and fury. In seconds, he had Alaric pinned beneath him, one hand clinched around his throat like an iron vise, the other palm flat on the ground beside his temple. Sweat gleamed on his flushed face. Alaric was trapped, neck securely fixed in place, so all he could do was stare up into the green eyes burning with raw, unrestrained anger.

"Never," Halden's voice was a low, scorching growl, breath hot on Alaric's skin, "underestimate me again."

Gods. He was beautiful.

Alaric *had* underestimated him, hadn't he? Not the man's skill— he'd known Halden was the finest knight at this tournament— but the depth beneath that brash exterior. The fire in those green eyes wasn't just temper; it was purpose. And here was the core of Halden's hurt, the thing that had made him the Upstart in the first place. Every victory was another piece of evidence that a commoner's blood could run just as noble as any lord's.

Alaric felt his breath catch as understanding dawned. This wasn't just some hot-headed peasant with talent. This was a man whose fury had direction, whose every move was calculated defiance against a world that dismissed him. He would never be as refined as Alaric, would never shake the roughness from himself, but gods, the intensity of Halden's yearning was. . .intoxicating.

Alaric knew he should say something cutting back, but blood hammered in his temples. And lower. His gaze drifted to Halden's hips—straddling him, pressing him down—and to that hand at his throat, possessive and strong. The heavy, relentless pressure of another body made his breathing shallow. But it wasn't just another body. It was the Upstart, a lightning bolt of brilliance in an otherwise boring existence, and Alaric's body trembled with a heat that pulsed in his groin, betraying him.

This was no simple sparring match. It was a collision of wills—and bodies—and Halden's thumb, ghosting along Alaric's pulse point, was sparking wildfire beneath his skin. A maddening sensation filled him, and lower, Alaric's groin throbbed with insolent insistence.

Halden froze as he sensed the stirring beneath him. His fierce gaze darted downward, widened in shock, then snapped back to Alaric's face. Still, he didn't shift.

Alaric slowed his breathing, chest rising and falling with deliberate control. Perhaps any other man would have felt shame, but Alaric was a creature of court; you learn quickly, in such a place, how to recognise a kindred spirit. The tension crackling between them wasn't just resentment, nor grudging respect.

And Halden wasn't moving. Not one inch. That refusal to recoil told Alaric exactly who he was.

He watched Halden's hips twitch, saw the unmistakable bulge straining at his breeches. Delight bloomed in Alaric's chest. He felt Halden's weight shift, the taut shoulders, the spark of awareness flaring in those green eyes. Was the Upstart ashamed of his own body?

Whether Halden could admit it or not, Alaric recognised his hunger. Halden was a man who wanted another man for the pure pleasure of conquest. Halden's eyes were wide, pupils blown with desire, and the hard length pressing through his breeches against Alaric's hip betrayed him completely. Gods, what a revelation—the Upstart might actually match him in bed as fiercely as he had in the lists. The thought made Alaric's breath catch, an unfamiliar flutter of anticipation beneath his practiced composure.

A slow, calculating smile curved Alaric's lips. Halden sat up straighter at the sight, a flicker of comprehension flaring in those verdant eyes.

"My tent," Alaric rasped, voice low and certain. "Tonight. Once the grounds lie silent. You can work out all your anger with me another way."

Halden's pupils dilated. His grip tightened for an infinitesimal instant, a real, learned rage wanting to choke the life out of Alaric for the suggestion. Alaric's heart raced at the thrill, at the sudden crushing pressure. But Halden quickly snatched his hand away. Alaric tentatively raised a leather glove to his neck.

Interesting indeed.

They lingered, locked in that frozen tableau, staring at one another until the dominance between them blurred beyond recognition. Alaric could no longer tell who was in control.

Finally, Halden broke away. He rolled free and vaulted to his feet, moving with the same urgency with which he'd felled Alaric in the first place. He didn't glance back; his retreating form was all rigid lines and simmering tension, and Alaric loved it.

When the Upstart had scurried off, Alaric lay still for a long moment, tasting the phantom weight of Halden's body imprinted on his skin. His breathing steadied, though the fire in his veins refused to die. When he finally rose and reclaimed his sword, his hands were steady; every part of him had been trained for such restraint.

But inside, something had fractured. A barrier had

crumbled, and his insides flared with eager hope, with promise.

What might it be like to be taken to bed by someone who truly desired him? Not the simpering courtiers with their every gasp calculated to please him, but someone who would challenge him thrust for thrust.

To match a man on the field was one thing, and to match that same man in bed another. Wouldn't it be delicious, Alaric wondered, to find a man that might challenge him in both regards?

The thought left him aching for nightfall.

7
HAL

Any sane man would not have left his tent that night.

So why, then, was Hal skirting across the dark tournament crowds like some common thief?

Sweat prickled at his hairline despite the cool night air, and his heart hammered against his chest, and no matter how loudly he called himself a fool and an idiot, Hal the Upstart did not stop walking.

He'd left Perrin sleeping. The boy had been exhausted from the day's work and had barely managed to eat before collapsing onto his pallet. He'd had every intention of joining his squire until he took to bed himself, and his idiot cock kept twitching at the memory of the Nameless Knight pinned beneath him. He hadn't consciously made the decision. It was his body's will. Hal had waited until the squire's breathing deepened and steadied, then slipped out without a word.

Now, Hal stopped ten feet from the tent's entrance. A muscle jumped in his jaw. His legs tensed, ready to flee back to his own tent. Surely that was the only way he could face Ser Alaric the Nameless tomorrow with his pride intact.

This was stupid. Reckless. He should be resting, should be focused, should be doing anything except walking toward a tent in the dead of night because some aristocratic bastard had looked at him with those silver eyes and said, *"my tent, tonight"*, like it was already decided.

But even now, heat was flooding him at the memory of Alaric craning to look at him. At the phantom sensation of Alaric's warm torso pressing against Hal's inner thighs. His cock hardened without sense, from the memory alone, and Hal pressed his forehead into his hand. Damn his body. Damn his desire. Damn it all to Hell.

The flap opened.

Alaric stood in the entrance, backlit by a single candle burning somewhere in the tent's interior. He was shirtless again, which distracted Hal fiercely, and his face was mostly shadow. But his eyes caught what little light there was and reflected it back—silver and knowing and entirely too satisfied. He'd been waiting. He'd known Hal would come.

"I was starting to think," Alaric said softly, "you'd lost your nerve."

Hal's jaw tightened. "I'm not—"

But Alaric's hand shot out, fingers closing around his wrist, and Hal was being pulled forward into the tent's dim interior. The canvas fell shut behind them, cutting off the night and the grounds and any possibility of retreat.

The space was smaller than Hal remembered from his earlier visit. Or maybe it just felt that way with Alaric standing so close, still gripping his wrist, his thumb pressed against Hal's pulse. Which was racing. Which Alaric now knew.

The single candle on the small camp table cast more shadow than light, turning Alaric into some hero carved from marble.

Hal was. . .a brute next to him. What was he doing here?

Alaric came close, and Hal pulled his face away.

"This doesn't mean anything," Hal grunted. He needed to establish that now, before things went further. Needed Alaric to understand that whatever happened in this tent stayed in this tent. "Tomorrow, I'm still going to beat you. Still going to take that championship and prove yesterday was a fucking fluke."

Alaric's smile widened. "Of course you are."

Hal scowled. The bastard was underestimating him again. Had he learned nothing?

Hal tried to pull his wrist free, but the other knight's grip held firm.

"I mean it," Hal insisted. It was a difficult thing, looking at Alaric this close up. "This changes nothing. You're still my opponent. Still the bastard who ended my streak."

"Mm." Alaric's free hand came up, fingers trailing along Hal's jaw with a lightness that made his skin prickle. "How admirable. Such fierce determination. Tell me, do you always need to convince yourself this thoroughly before you take what you want?"

"I don't—" But the denial died as Alaric's thumb brushed across his lower lip. He swallowed. Heat shot through him, pooling low in his belly, and his breathing went shallow without his permission.

"You don't what?" Alaric's voice dropped lower, intimate in a way that made the tent feel smothering. His eyes were large and bold with his intentions; Alaric was not pretending the way Hal was. "Want this? Want me? Because your body's telling a different story, Ser Hal."

The bastard was right. Hal felt his cock hard against the rough linen of his breeches, his body coiling with a hunger. This damn stranger with his bright smile had him on edge, and Alaric was staring at him with a knowing smile set to drive Hal mad.

But Alaric was beautiful because he was bred that way. Hal wasn't blind; it wasn't his fault his body was attracted to someone so perfect. Hal didn't have to like Alaric to admit that.

Hal didn't have to like him to use his body that night.

"Shut up," he growled and slammed into Alaric. Their mouths collided harshly. Alaric's mouth opened under his, breath catching in a sharp exhale.

He shoved until Alaric's shoulders hit the tent pole with a muffled thud.

Alaric laughed low, hands clamping Hal's broad shoulders and hauling him closer—hard muscle against muscle, the scratch of stubble against his jaw igniting him like spark to tinder. A gleeful, excited shiver shot up Hal's spine. Alaric lacked a woman's warmth, but he was all firm muscle and edge and infuriating smile, and he was a brilliant jouster, and that was somehow better than him being some pretty girl. Hal, who enjoyed most anyone's company, loved this particular heat: this man had thrown him on his back, but Hal could have him with his legs in the air now, if he wanted it. And wanted it, he did. Suddenly, Hal was rutting against Alaric without a care, their cocks rubbing against one another through their breeches.

When they parted to gasp, Alaric's lips were wet and swollen. "Was that so hard?"

He didn't like it when Alaric talked to him like that. Hated the condescension, the pity-filled looks. Alaric wanted this as much as he did—more, since he'd been the one to so eagerly summon Hal here tonight. Yes, that was it—that was the edge Hal needed to win *this* bout. Alaric might have been quick-witted and good with his words, but Hal had always been good with his hands.

So he shut the other knight up. Hal lunged again, teeth grazing Alaric's lower lip, slamming their mouths together with more force, more need. Alaric answered blow for blow, one hand threading into Hal's hair and yanking so hard the tension bit into his scalp. Pain grounded him. He growled low, and they stumbled back toward Alaric's cot.

Hal's fingers found the ties of Alaric's breeches, tugging until fabric fell away in ragged strips. The knight laughed, breath coming fast, eyes glinting in the lamplight as they fell onto the cot, limbs knotting together.

"Eager," Alaric teased, though he himself was already working at Hal's breeches. "That little squire of yours must not be serving his knight in—"

"I said shut up." Hal bit down on that pouty lower lip, hard enough to draw a sharp gasp from the highborn slut. Alaric went still, swallowed, and for the first time, it was him losing control.

But Alaric recovered too quickly, and he rolled them both deftly. Hal's back hit the cot and Alaric settled between his thighs. The reversal happened so fast that Hal barely registered it before those clever hands were pulling his shirt over his head, baring his chest to the tent's cool air.

"How'd you manage that?" Hal grunted. "You're half my size."

But Alaric hadn't heard him. His eyes were heavy, his

mouth opened, and he breathed hard as his eyes dragged up Hal's chest.

"Fuck," Alaric breathed. Hal had never heard the nobleman swear, and the raw appreciation in his voice made Hal's cock throb. Long fingers traced the scars scattered across his torso—souvenirs from years of training, from before Hal had learned to protect himself properly. "You're magnificent."

That word lodged in Hal's chest. He barely knew how to make sense of it when applied to him; no one had ever called him that. Useful, yes. Strong, certainly. But magnificent? That was a word for noblemen and their fine horses, not for common-born knights with crooked noses and too many scars.

The way Alaric looked at him, heavy-lidded eyes dragging over Hal's form, dredged something ugly from the pit of Hal's stomach. No—absolutely not. He couldn't afford to think on that, didn't know how to handle the strange emotion he felt when this stranger so openly admired his body. So he grabbed Alaric's face and pulled him down into another bruising kiss, swallowing whatever other observations the knight might have offered.

"Don't fuck men like me in your high tower?" he grunted against Alaric's ear as he moved to sit in Hal's lap.

"And dirty my reputation?" Alaric quipped back. "Certainly not."

But he was flushed and rolling his hips, hard length brushing Hal's belly; how he managed to feign restraint when he was coming undone was anybody's guess.

"Oh, yeah?" Hal licked up Alaric's neck and quivered at the other man's moan. "What's got you so eager to get down into the muck now?"

"Only the hope," Alaric said, tilting his neck back down to meet Hal's eye, "that you'll keep up with me here as you do in the lists."

Well, fuck.

Their hips rocked together; cloth-covered friction that wasn't nearly enough, but still drew a groan from both of them. Gods, it had been a while since he'd fucked anything, hadn't it? A camp follower a handful of months ago, Perrin's mouth sometimes, and then the rough surface of his own palm. Had he ever had a lover push back against him with such eagerness? Such force? Had he ever had a lover wrestle him for damn control? It was like trying to sit on a wild horse, the way Alaric moved atop him. Hal's hands found Alaric's ass and squeezed, pulling him closer and grinding up against him.

Later, maybe, he'd be mortified by how quickly *he'd* fallen apart. Hal was all grunting animal, no knightly man in sight. But right now, all he could focus on was the heat building between them, the way Alaric's breath ghosted across his lips, the sounds the knight made when Hal's teeth found his throat.

Fuck this teasing. Hal flipped them again, using his weight advantage to pin Alaric beneath him and kill any chance the lithe knight would slip free. This time, when the knight laughed, it sounded surprised and pleased, and maybe a little bit hungry.

When Alaric reached down to Hal's breeches, Hal shifted back onto his haunches, giving Alaric more access. The other knight sat up eagerly, eyes bright and tongue pressed to the corner of his pink mouth as he undid the knot. Then he was pushing the breeches down over Hal's hips until his swollen cock sprang free. The cool air against the tender flesh of his cock made Hal hiss. A slickness coated the head already. Hal watched Alaric's eyes, watched as they softened and drifted away to someplace primal and old. Hal's anger was forgotten. He was only a man, or perhaps only a beast, and all of him wanted Alaric; wanted every part of the other knight. Then Alaric's hand wrapped around him, and all conscious thought fled.

"Gods," Hal choked out. The grip was firm, not choking; Alaric knew exactly how much pressure to apply, and Hal thrust into it without meaning to. His hips moved on instinct, chasing the sensation, while his mind spun out in a dozen different directions.

This was wrong. This was exactly what he needed. This was going to ruin him for tomorrow's match. This was the only thing that had felt right in days.

"Let me," Alaric said. There was a heavy, lulling desire in his voice that made Hal's knees weak. "Let me taste you."

The words went straight to Hal's cock. He moaned, rolled his neck forward and exhaled hot air over his own chest. The thought of Alaric's mouth on him. . .! The thought of using that aristocratic throat for his pleasure after the man it belonged to had humiliated him. . .!

Hal glanced up. Alaric's smile had turned wicked. But, Hell, Hal didn't have to be asked twice: he lay back, and Alaric shifted down the cot, positioning himself between Hal's thighs. The first wet heat of Alaric's mouth made Hal's vision blur at the edges, his back arching off the cot with a strangled, airy sound.

"Fuck," Hal gasped, fingers clawing at the blanket beneath him. He'd been sucked before, been sucked well, but Alaric was a nobleman, and here he was, dutifully servicing common-born Hal. Hal looked down and saw that pretty face, mouth distended around his cock, Alaric's bright eyes peering up at him through long lashes. . .shit. Alaric took him deeper, silver eyes flicking upward to watch Hal's face as his throat worked around him. The knight's tongue traced patterns that made Hal's thighs tremble. He was good. He must have done this before, many times.

Alaric pulled back just enough to circle the head with agonising precision, eyes locked on Hal's to read his expression. Sweat slicked Alaric's aristocratic throat, his pulse visible beneath skin that had likely never known a day's labour. Yet here he was—silver eyes clouded with lust, breath coming in ragged gasps no different from anyone else Hal had bedded. The realisation that desire made equals of them both, that even this highborn knight could be reduced to animal need, sent heat coursing through Halden's veins like strong wine.

Alaric licked the head once more. Hal's hand slammed onto the back of Alaric's head and forced him down in one fluid motion. Alaric swallowed him, the vibration of the knight's appreciative moan travelling through Hal's cock straight to his spine. Fuck yes. Hal kept a fistful of Alaric's hair in his palm. Almost in response, Alaric brought his strong hands up to grip Hal's hips, thumbs pressing into the hollows beside his hipbones, holding him open and exposed.

Hal couldn't look away. Couldn't stop watching those aristocratic lips stretched around him, couldn't stop the helpless roll of his hips when Alaric relaxed his throat and took him impossibly deeper. Alaric devoured him like he was starving for it. He bobbed Alaric's head up and down like the other knight, this beautiful man, was a toy entirely for his pleasure, and—

"Stop," Hal choked out, tangling his fingers in Alaric's dark curls. His body trembled on the knife's edge—if he had any hope of lasting, he needed Alaric off him. Immediately. But the knight kept bloody teasing him, licking and sucking, so Hal yanked Alaric's head up by his hair. The knight hissed in pain, but when he grabbed Alaric's shoulders and flipped their bodies again, a delighted laugh escaped his lips, beautiful alabaster skin flushing red. Alaric let himself be manhandled into position. All the while, Hal was trying to catch his breath—and some sense of himself.

"You're damn good at that," Hal grunted as he tugged down Alaric's breeches with shaking hands. He'd never done this before—never even considered it, not even with Perrin. But Perrin was his squire; there was nothing there except obligation. Alaric wanted him, and even if it was born from some twisted competitive flair, Hal wanted him, too. He wanted to see what Alaric looked like, what colour that flushed head would be, the size and shape of him, his taste. . .

"What can I say?" Alaric purred. "A silver tongue is a boon at court."

"Court," Hal sneered. "You nobles are as filthy as us commoners."

With that, Hal pulled Alaric's breeches down. The knight's cock sprang free, throbbing as it bounced. Hal moaned to himself; of course, this was fucking perfect, too. Hal stared at it for a moment, at the blushed pink tip, at the way it pulsed, the pleasing width and slight upward curse. His mind was a drowned out distant thing, and there was only this lustful, red-faced knight with his twitching cock, waiting for Hal's mouth.

Only, he'd never done it before. Uncertainty warred with his desire; he glanced up at Alaric, who was breathing hard.

Thing was, Hal liked being good at things. Still, he'd

been shit at jousting when he started. Hadn't been good at much of anything straight off the mark. It was only that Alaric was an expert that made him nervous; another thing Alaric was better at.

But this, too, he could learn; he could come to excel at. But first he had to try. And he'd be an eager student; he wanted Alaric to lose that pristine mask completely.

"I'm out of practice," he murmured, taking Alaric's cock in hand. It was a white lie he hoped would cover any blunders. Alaric peered down at him, mouth working to reply, but before he could, Hal experimentally licked out over the head.

Alaric shifted with a gasp, and encouraged, Hal relaxed and pressed both his body and mouth lower. Still, he knew he was an amateur. He couldn't find the rhythm Alaric had made look effortless. His teeth scraped once, and Alaric hissed, though his hand in Hal's hair tightened rather than pushed him away. But gradually Hal figured it out—how much saliva he needed, how much suction to use, where to put his tongue, how to breathe through his nose when Alaric's hips thrust up and pushed deeper into his throat.

"God," Alaric breathed above him. "Yes, just like that. You're doing so well."

The praise went straight to Hal's cock. Hell, you can raise a commoner to knighthood, but you can't change their blood, and Hal had been raised to seek out praise from his betters. Apparently, that fucking training had stuck. Praise felt good to him, felt right—he enjoyed hearing it enough to try hard, in the hopes he'd receive more of it.

He rubbed himself against the bed for relief and let himself enjoy what he was doing. He hollowed his cheeks, taking Alaric deeper, losing himself in the salt-musk taste and the weight on his tongue. Somewhere in this stretch of time, where he was wetly sucking and Alaric's sharp hips were thrusting up to meet him, his mind raced ahead until he could almost feel what it would be like to sink himself into Alaric's ass.

He rolled with the fantasy of being inside Alaric, to have the knight beneath him, legs spread wide, taking Hal's cock the way Hal was taking his now. He imagined Alaric's face twisted in pleasure, in gruff pain, those silver eyes glazed and desperate. Yes, Hal would undo all the sharp smugness from the aristocrat's face. Wouldn't it be a shameful thing, a humiliation, to enjoy getting fucked by a crass upstart such as him? The fantasy made him moan around Alaric's length, the vibration drawing a sharp gasp from above.

Hal's hand wrapped around the base, stroking what he couldn't fit in his mouth. He pulled back to lap at the head, savouring the bitter fluid there, before swallowing him down again with newfound hunger.

But when he pulled up to breathe, the world flipped again.

Alaric moved with surprising strength, using his legs to hook around Hal's shoulders and roll them until their positions were reversed. Hal found himself on his back with Alaric straddling his chest, that wet aristocratic cock pointed directly at his face.

Before he could process the reversal, Alaric slapped his cock against Hal's cheek—once, twice—leaving wet trails across his stubbled skin.

Hal's chest lurched, though the emotion behind it was muddy. Unclear. Gone was the certainty he was in control, but in its place wasn't anger. He placed his hands on Alaric's ass and gasped, realising how intently Alaric watched him.

"Beautiful," Alaric murmured, stroking himself slowly.

Up and down, slick and swollen. The casual dominance stunned Hal, who fell into a kind of trance watching the motion. The way the foreskin moved, the way the glans emerged, slick and flushed, and *fuck,* why did it feel like the sun itself was in his chest as he watched the other knight touch himself?

Alaric used his other hand to grip Hal's jaw. They locked eyes. Alaric tilted his head and let go of him, rocking forward so that every forward thrust scraped the head of his cock against Hal's parted lips.

"You look so good like this," Alaric told him. "So desperate. So eager to please."

Heat flooded Hal's face, embarrassment mixing with arousal. He made to shove away, to reclaim some dignity, but the knight's free hand was pinning him down. Alaric rubbed his tip against Hal's lips, and all the fight guttered out, so when Alaric next guided himself forward, Hal surrendered utterly.

Fuck it. This was... so ...

He opened his mouth and took Alaric inside.

"Good," Alaric hissed. His voice dropped into an intimate register; he was half whispering to himself. "That's it, Ser Halden. Yes."

It was the use of his title that had Hal's eyes rolling back. He felt his throat open, head fogging with a kind of pathetic pleasure. Alaric took advantage, thrusting deep into Hal's throat until he choked, then pulling all the way out with a moan. Hal coughed and spluttered, stringy saliva coating his lips, and Alaric stared like he wanted to hold Hal down by the neck and use his throat mercilessly. The way Hal had intended to ruin Alaric.

But instead, Alaric only gracefully rolled off him and

onto his side. He stared up at Hal, his other hand moving low to stroke Hal's ignored, aching cock.

Hal threw his head back, all his frustration vanishing.

"Feels good?" Alaric murmured.

"Of course," Hal whispered.

Hal looked at him, brow furrowed.

"Do you want to feel me?" Alaric asked. Hal dipped his eyes to Alaric's hand; he was feeling him now, wasn't he? Then Alaric murmured, "Do you want to feel how warm my insides are around your cock?"

Hal's eyes fluttered closed. A dizziness struck him, a momentary loss of awareness. He couldn't find the will to reply, either; what would come out if not a desperate litany of *yes, yes, yes*?

Alaric let go, and now Hal's eyes snapped opened with an exasperated hiss. Alaric, if he noticed, ignored Hal's over eagerness and pushed his legs apart with gentle but inexorable pressure. Hal felt suddenly vulnerable like that, with Alaric's eyes drinking him in and his legs spread to either side. What had happened that Alaric was taking control? How was it that Alaric could be blunt about what position he would take, and yet Hal was the one spread legged now?

Alaric ran a teasing hand over Hal's cock. "You want this. Want me. Say it."

Hal couldn't. "Fuck you," he managed, but the words came out breathless. Pathetic.

"Mm. Eventually." Alaric flashed him a gentle smile. That confirmation—Gods, it would happen. Gods, he'd get to fuck the smug bastard—made Hal knock his head back against the pillow.

Alaric continued, "I was considering straddling you right now. Riding you until you were screaming."

Hal's head swam with the vision that assaulted him;

Alaric's lean musculature bouncing on his cock, holding Hal down to get his own pleasure. It wasn't quite the reclamation of power Hal had imagined for himself—not quite as hot as fucking his better into the mattress until the other man screamed—but he felt his hips tilt up all the same. Alaric noticed too, and finally his hand wrapped around Hal's cock again, stroking in slow, long arcs.

"But first, I'm going to make you beg for it. Going to reduce you to nothing but need. And tomorrow, when you're trying to concentrate on the joust, you're going to remember exactly how you fell apart for me."

Hal sneered. "You fucking—"

Alaric's mouth returned to his cock, and whatever semi-coherent argument had been brewing became stupidly irrelevant. Hal fell back and closed his eyes with a high-pitched moan. This time it was different; he couldn't even think to be embarrassed. Alaric took his time, alternating between long, slow sucks and quick flicks of his tongue that had Hal writhing. His hands roamed everywhere—pinching Hal's nipples, squeezing his thighs, pressing against places that made Hal's back arch off the cot. Every part of Hal's body felt suddenly made for pleasure. Not pain, as he'd always thought. There was more to his physicality than jousting; more to his worth than what honour he might bring a noble house. There was his body—the use of his body—for whatever he wanted. And he fucking *wanted*. . .!

"Please," Hal heard himself gasp. "Please, I need—"

"Need what?" Alaric pulled off just enough to speak, his breath ghosting over Hal's wet cock. "Tell me what you need."

But before Hal could answer—before he could put into

words the desperate ache building in his body—the tent flap opened.

Hal jerked at the movement. Perrin stood in the entrance, his thin frame backlit by dying campfires. His face was a study in shock, dark eyes wide and mouth slightly open as he took in the scene before him. Hal knew what he was seeing: his knight on his back, naked and hard and obviously debauched. Alaric between his legs, equally naked, his lips still wet with Hal's precum.

For a moment, nobody moved. The tableau held frozen, three men caught in a moment that couldn't be explained away or ignored.

Then Alaric laughed.

It wasn't the pleased chuckle Hal had heard this evening, but something cold and sharp and calculated. He had been edging from stranger to lover, but the sound re-established the gulf between them.

"I think your pet is in love with you, Ser Hal." Alaric climbed off the cot with leisurely grace. He made no attempt to cover himself, completely unashamed. "Perhaps you should go tend to him."

Hal scrambled upright, his mind struggling to process what was happening. Perrin just stood there, staring, his face cycling through expressions Hal had no names for. How dare he—how dare Perrin stand there and look hurt!

"Perrin," Hal started, reaching for his breeches with shaking hands. It came out trembling, like Hal was about to apologise. He shook his own head, mouth running dry. But it was fury he felt. An embarrassed rage. "The fuck are you standing there for, boy? Leave us."

Perrin, who had been obedient as long as Hal had known him, did not move.

"S-sorry, ser."

Sorry, he said, and still, he did not move.

Alaric was pulling on his own clothes now, and the moment—a small, blissful moment of real pleasure—was disappearing. Fuck Perrin right in the ass.

The young man raised his chin. Wait—Hal had been wrong; it wasn't hurt in his eyes, but fear. Perrin glanced at him, then fixed his gaze on the back of the tent.

"I think. . .h-he's using you, ser."

Hal blinked at him. "What?"

"I think I know," Perrin whispered, "who he is."

Alaric's head lifted very slowly, but something about the movement made Hal's blood run cold. The warmth that had filled the tent moments ago drained away, replaced by a creeping horror as Alaric turned to face him. His silver eyes were cold as stone, holding no trace of the heat they'd shown before.

Hal was looking at Alaric, but he was seeing the Nameless Knight. Alaric didn't look away as he asked Perrin, "And who do you think I am?"

"Lord Vaelor's son."

There was no twitch of recognition in Alaric's face, but he was a good liar, wasn't he? Hal shifted his gaze to Perrin.

"You making this up, Perrin?"

Perrin's lips pinched together. "An educated guess, ser. I—was worried."

"So you came to find me?" Hal hissed at his squire. Was this an act of care from his squire, or something petty? Hal risked a glance back at Alaric. Whatever it was, scolding the squire here in front of his rival wasn't safe. Leaving would be the best move, and instead he wet his lips and nodded to Perrin. "Fine. Tell me the story."

Perrin straightened. "Lord Vaelor was a border lord who fell out of royal favour two years ago after he was accused of raising arms without leave. After he was charged for treason, his eldest son vanished from court. It would make sense," Perrin said firmly, "for him to be so interested in besting you, with your common birth. He reasserts the old order and begins to clear his name."

Hal considered this. Alaric's face still betrayed nothing. "So, what? You think he plans to reveal his name tomorrow? He wants to beat me again to announce his newfound path?" Hal asked.

"You should leave now," Alaric said, and his educated accent had sharpened into something almost cruel. But something passed in his eyes—what? If only Hal could read emotions as well as he could a knight's jousting tells. "Both of you. This," Alaric gestured rapidly between Perrin and Hal, "has been illuminating."

Hal had just gotten his breeches on but couldn't seem to make his hands work well enough to lace them. "Listen," he said, turning to Alaric. "My squire is as damn forward as me. But if you are Lord Vaelor's son, fucking me won't—"

"Did you really think," Alaric interrupted, his smile turning cold, "that I wanted you here for any reason other than tomorrow's match? That I invited you to my tent out of genuine desire rather than strategy?"

A cold knot formed in Hal's stomach. He shut his mouth, felt himself close and retreat back to the safety of his anger, his volatility.

And still, because he could never learn, he muttered, "I don't—"

"You don't understand?" Alaric's eyebrow rose, aristocratic and contemptuous. "With your breeding, of course not. So, let me make it simple for you, then. Tomorrow we face each other in the finals. I needed an advantage. And you—" His gaze raked over Hal's half-naked form with something that looked like disdain. "—you were so eager, all I had to do was suggest it."

No. No, that wasn't. . . He shook his head. That couldn't be true. The way Alaric had looked at him. . .could desire like that be forced?

"You said you wanted to prove your worth without your name," Hal hissed. "Was that a lie?"

But if Alaric heard him, he ignored Hal's word. Alaric finished dressing and turned to face both of them fully. "Tell me, Ser Hal—do you think you'll fight well tomorrow, pent up as you are? With your body aching and your mind replaying every sound you made, every desperate plea? Because I certainly won't have that problem."

The cruelty of it stole Hal's breath. Even if Alaric was lying, even if he wasn't who Perrin thought, this was the same ugly brand of hate every noble had thrown his way. Hal had lived in the shadow of this muck his whole life. Was Alaric embarrassed? Was embarrassment enough of a reason for—for *this?* What a petty asshole.

Fuck. Fuck it all.

Hal looked at Perrin, whose face had gone carefully blank in the way it did when he was trying not to feel anything at all, and shame burned through Hal like fire.

Because it didn't matter if Alaric was lying, then. He was right about one thing: Hal would be thinking about this for quite some time.

"Get out," Alaric said, his voice final. "And thank your squire for providing such a timely interruption. I was starting to worry I'd have to find another way to end this before things went too far."

Hal's hands curled into fists. Part of him wanted to hit Alaric, wanted to wipe that cold smile off his face and make him hurt the way Hal was hurting. But Perrin was already retreating from the tent, and the sight of his squire's thin shoulders hunched against the night air broke something in Hal's chest.

He grabbed his shirt and stumbled toward the entrance, unable to look at either of them. Behind him, Alaric's laugh followed—soft and satisfied and entirely devoid of warmth.

"See you tomorrow, Ser Hal. I do hope you'll still give me a good match."

8
PERRIN

The tent smelled of sweat when Perrin returned to it, though he quickly realised he was smelling himself; his anxiety, pushing out of his pores. His hands wouldn't stop shaking—hadn't stopped since he'd turned away from the Nameless Knight's canvas walls, since the image of Hal sprawled and wanting beneath another man had burned itself into his vision like a brand. He stood just inside the entrance of their shared tent, one hand gripping the support pole because his legs threatened betrayal and tried to breathe through the thing lodged in his chest.

He'd known, hadn't he? Some part of him had understood where Hal was going when the knight had slipped out after dark. Perrin had woken immediately, and he should have gone back to sleep. He should have given his knight whatever privacy he'd been seeking in the darkness.

Instead, he'd followed. Like a dog trailing its master. Like a fool who couldn't leave well enough alone.

The single candle he'd left burning had melted down to a stub. Its flame was guttering, threatening to go out entirely. In the low light, shadows pooled in the tent's corners, making the familiar space feel foreign. The armour stand loomed like a silent witness to Perrin's overreach. The carefully maintained pieces of Hal's gear gleamed dully in the weak light, each one a testament to Perrin's devotion, his endless service, his absolute stupidity in thinking any of it mattered beyond function.

What had he been thinking, storming in like that? He was a squire. A *squire!* But no matter how he tried to dislodge the memories, he kept seeing Hal's broad chest, muscles flexing. The Nameless Knight between his thighs, dark hair spilling over Hal's hip. The sounds—Gods, the sounds Hal had been making. Desperate and raw and nothing like the careful control he maintained during the day. Perrin had heard those sounds and felt something tear in his chest, felt the careful architecture of his world collapse into rubble.

Because he'd wanted to be the one making Hal sound like that.

He had serviced Hal before, but only occasionally, and often when Hal had no other choice. Even then, Hal had only used his mouth and been quick about it, like he was desperate to be away as soon as he was finished. He made no noise beyond a quick grunt when he came. After what Perrin had seen tonight, whatever he'd given Hal those times couldn't be called real pleasure.

Despite their arrangement, they had managed a careful distance; Perrin had only been providing another service as Hal's squire. It was mostly Perrin who'd had to pretend his hands didn't linger when adjusting armour or that his pulse didn't quicken when Hal emerged from the bath, water still beading on his shoulders. He'd spent years telling himself that loyalty and devotion were sufficient, that he didn't need more, that wanting more was a betrayal of everything their relationship was built on.

And then the Nameless Knight had arrived, and within two days Hal had been in his tent, in his bed, giving him everything Perrin had spent years not asking for.

Footsteps outside. Heavy. Uneven. Hal's gait, but off balance.

Perrin straightened, released the tent pole, and forced his hands to stop their trembling. When Hal pushed through the entrance, Perrin immediately dropped his head in a bow, but not before he saw Ser Hal's expression.

His jaw was set so tightly, Perrin could see the muscle jumping beneath the skin, which was Hal's usual tell. Some stormy emotion raged in him. His eyes—those green eyes that could go from furious to pleased in a heartbeat—were flat and cold as river stones. He'd dressed hastily; his shirt was half-unlaced, his breeches loose at the waist, his hair still mussed from another man's hands.

He looked betrayed, and Perrin had been the one to betray him.

"I'm sorry, Ser Halden," Perrin said quietly. "I shouldn't have—I should have stayed here. Should have given you privacy."

Hal said nothing. His silence was harder to bear than anger; it pressed down on Perrin's shoulders like a physical weight, demanding he explain, justify, apologise again for the unforgivable sin of witnessing his knight's humiliation.

"I woke up, and you were gone," Perrin continued, still not looking up. "I was concerned. Thought perhaps you'd taken ill, or—" The lie died on his tongue. He couldn't do it. Couldn't pretend this was innocent concern rather than the jealous trailing of someone who had no right to jealousy. "I'm sorry," he repeated, because what else could he say?

Only the truth. "I guessed where you were and what was happening. I guessed, too, who he was. And you were right, I can't be sure about it, and I didn't know if he really *was* using you, and it's not that you're not attractive, but I didn't want you to wake up tomorrow with regret, and I—"

"Stop."

The word cracked like a whip. Perrin's head came up automatically, years of obedience overriding his need to defend himself. Hal stood with his fists clenched at his sides, his whole body rigid with suppressed violence. But it wasn't directed at Perrin. No, Perrin knew Hal's rage and had weathered it often. This was. . .internal. Or aimed at the Nameless Knight. At the universe for putting him in a position where his squire had watched him be used and discarded like a training dummy.

"Don't apologise," Hal said, each word ground out through clenched teeth. "Don't fucking apologise to me when I'm the one who—" He cut himself off, turned away, pressed both palms against the tent's support pole as if he, too, needed something to hold him upright. His shoulders rose and fell with harsh breaths.

Perrin stayed quiet, letting Hal work through whatever he needed to work through. That was part of his job too: Knowing when to speak and when silence served better.

Tomorrow, Hal would face the Nameless Knight in the tournament finals. Tomorrow, he would need to be sharp, focused, capable of the precision that had carried him through so long undefeated. Tomorrow, he would need to be the best version of himself.

Tonight, he was a man coming apart at the seams.

Perrin's mind shifted, practical instincts overriding hurt feelings. He'd seen Hal like this before—wound so tight he couldn't think straight, his body vibrating with unused violence and energy and lacking a place to put it. Usually, it happened before important bouts, when the stakes were high, and the pressure mounted. Perrin had learned how to handle it, how to offer what Hal needed without making it obvious the knight was being managed.

But this was different. This wasn't pre-bout nerves or the weight of expectation. This was rage and shame and self-loathing all tangled together, and beneath it—Perrin could see it in the set of Hal's shoulders, in the way he held himself, and in the tenting of his breeches—arousal that hadn't been fully satisfied. The Nameless Knight had gotten him worked up and then dismissed him, leaving him hanging with nowhere to put all that energy.

Hal would never sleep tonight. Gods, Perrin knew him: He would spend the hours until dawn replaying every moment in that tent, every word the Nameless Knight had said, every touch and taste and broken gasp. He would torture himself with it until his mind was too fractured to function properly.

And then tomorrow he would lose. Ser Halden would hand the championship to the man who'd used him.

Perrin couldn't allow that.

He moved forward, closing the distance between them with careful steps. Hal didn't turn, but his shoulders tensed further as Perrin came to stand just behind him. This close, Perrin could feel the heat radiating from him, could smell the sweat and sex that still clung to him. His stomach lurched.

"Ser Halden," Perrin said softly. "Please look at me."

For a moment, he thought Hal wouldn't comply. Then, slowly, the knight turned. His jaw was gritted, and a gleam in his eye threatened tears, though beneath, his green eyes glazed with fury. But under that, too, was just a man. The man Perrin cared for; a raw, wanting, utterly lost young man, just like Perrin himself.

Perrin met that gaze steadily. Let Hal see whatever he needed to see. Then, deliberately, he sank to his knees.

He decided, in himself, that this wasn't submission. It wasn't like those other times when Ser Halden had no other choice, and Perrin was only performing his duty. This was something Perrin wanted to do; to give Hal pleasure and release, and in a way, to set things right. This was an apology for witnessing his humiliation. This was a return to the proper dynamic. Perrin's place was on his knees before his knight, and Ser Halden should use his squire. Perrin did this not out of duty, but out of love.

He tilted his head back, exposing the long line of his throat. Hal's eyes tracked the movement, something dark and hungry flickering across his features. His mouth parted, but he said nothing.

So Perrin provided.

"You'll lose your edge in tomorrow's tilt if you don't release this," Perrin said. Boldly, he reached out and pressed his hands on either side of Hal's groin, gently squeezing the firm quad muscle there. His voice was steady despite the way his heart hammered against his ribs. "You know you will. You're wound too tight. Too far in your own head."

Hal's jaw worked. His hands clenched and unclenched at his sides. "Perrin—"

"You need this." Perrin kept his gaze locked on Hal's face, refused to look away even as heat flooded his cheeks. "Let me help you. That's my job, isn't it? To make sure you're ready for tomorrow."

Maybe in part it was true. Yes, preparing Hal was his job. But this act was about Perrin claiming something for himself, about inserting himself into the space the Nameless Knight had occupied. He would prove, even if only to himself, that he could give Hal what that aristocratic bastard had only pretended to offer.

Hal stared down at him. Then, finally, he exhaled, a long breath that seemed to carry some of the tension out with it. His hand came up, fingers threading through Perrin's dark hair. The grip was gentle at first, almost tentative, as if he was giving Perrin one last chance to pull away. Perrin didn't. Then Hal's fingers tightened in a possessive grip, and his other hand came to rest against Perrin's jaw.

Hal slipped his thumb into Perrin's mouth, pressed against his tongue. Perrin closed his lips around it, and Hal nodded down at him. Very slowly, he slid the slick digit out and gazed down at Perrin with heavy eyes.

"You're sure?" Hal murmured.

Perrin felt his mind tilt toward that blissful place; sometimes, surrendering to Hal made him feel close to the heavens. He knew, tonight, his knight would take him there. "I'm sure. Let me take care of you."

The words were barely out before Hal's hand fisted in his hair, yanking Perrin's head forward. Perrin's breath caught, shooting surprise and arousal through him in equal measure. Hal's other hand worked at the laces of his half-undone breeches with shaking fingers, and Perrin realised with a jolt that his knight was nervous.

Perrin reached up, covered Hal's fumbling hands with his own. "Let me," he murmured, and set to work on the laces with the same efficiency he brought to armour maintenance. The breeches parted, and Hal's cock sprang free—still half-hard from whatever the Nameless Knight had started, thick and flushed and leaking.

Perrin's mouth watered. He'd never done this in the light before, the pair of them always having moved in the dark to preserve some pretence of their dynamic. But now, seeing Hal's body in truth, seeing the way it twitched and how Hal looked down at him, Perrin knew he wanted this.

He leaned forward, pressed his lips to the base of Hal's cock, and felt the knight's entire body go rigid above him.

Hal let out a soft moan. Perrin took his time, taking Hal's cock in his right hand and angling it away. That gave him a deeper range, and he leaned in to lick over Hal's balls. The knight jolted, but he made no sound yet. Perrin felt determined to earn a real noise out of Ser Halden this time, and so, he teased Hal's poor, edged cock: slowly licking up the underside, tonguing the prominent vein, and then dragging his tongue over the slit. Then Hal whimpered, this high, beautiful sound that made Perrin moan in turn. What power he had suddenly, at that moment, was more than he'd ever possessed in his life.

Then he opened his mouth and sucked at the reddened head, sucked until saliva coated his mouth. He pooled it over Hal's cock and slicked it over the length with his hands, and as Hal whispered above him—a breathy chorus of *yes, yes*—Perrin began to slide down Hal's length inch by careful inch. He went until the head bumped the back of his throat, and he had to suppress a gag. But Hal moaned at the choked sound, and those strong hands came down to press Perrin in place. Perrin had no choice but to adjust his body and open up his throat, even as his jaw ached and his eyes watered. But he was a good squire, wasn't he? All he wanted was to please his knight.

Perrin knew Hal liked him to stay low, to sink all the way down, to move steadily. And as Perrin moved, Hal's hand tightened in his hair, and the sound he made—low and broken and utterly desperate—told Perrin he was doing something right.

He pulled back, sucked at the head, tasted salt and musk and something uniquely Hal. His tongue explored the ridge, the sensitive spot just beneath, and Hal's hips jerked forward involuntarily. Gagging again, Perrin steadied himself with hands on Hal's thighs, feeling the muscles bunch and flex beneath his palms.

"Fuck," Hal gasped. His other hand came down to cup Perrin's jaw. "Good–boy," he grunted, heavy-lidded eyes drinking Perrin in. That freely given praise made Perrin moan. His eyebrows crashed together, heat rushing to his groin, and he went limp with it—praise was all he ever wanted, all he ever needed. He'd endure it all to be Hal's good boy.

Perrin, his own groin ignored, spread his legs involuntarily as he sank lower on Hal's cock. He found a rhythm, shallow thrusts that let him breathe between, and focused on the sounds Hal was making. Each gasp and groan were a revelation, proof that Perrin was affecting him, that he had power here despite being on his knees.

Soon, Hal's breathing went ragged. He gripped Perrin's head and moved him like he was nothing, thrusting deeper and deeper into Perrin's mouth until thick saliva was pooling at the corners of his lips. Perrin grunted and moaned, letting his eyes roll back as he succumbed to Hal's force. He was a vessel for Hal's pleasure, and it felt right, it felt *good.*

Ser Hal's hips moved with increasing urgency, and Perrin let him, opened his throat and took it, felt tears streaming down his face from the effort, but refused to pull away. He wanted this. Wanted to give Hal release. Wanted to taste him, to swallow him down, to be the one who put that shattered look on his face.

"Perrin," Hal warned, his voice strangled. "I'm going to —if you don't want—"

But Perrin just looked up at him, maintaining eye contact even as Hal fucked deeper into his mouth, and that was apparently all the answer needed. Hal's grip turned almost painful, his body going rigid, and then he was coming with a choked-off shout, head thrown back to the heavens.

Warmth spluttered into Perrin's mouth. He moaned and swallowed convulsively as Hal's cock pulsed on his tongue, each spasm matched by the knight's harsh breathing above him. When it finally subsided, Perrin pulled off carefully and sat back on his shins, wiping his mouth with the back of his hand.

Hal stood above him, chest heaving, his face flushed, and eyes glazed. His touch was light against Perrin's cheek. For a moment, they just looked at each other—knight and squire, master and shadow, two men seeking pleasure in the dead of night.

Then Hal's knees buckled, and he sank down beside Perrin. His hand came up to cup the back of Perrin's neck, pulling him close until their foreheads touched. His breath ghosted across Perrin's lips, still ragged but slower now, coming back under control.

"Thank you," Hal whispered, and in them Perrin heard something beyond simple gratitude.

He closed his eyes and drooped against Hal's strong body, let himself feel the warmth of his knight pressed against him, the gentle pressure of fingers on his neck, and the intimacy of shared breath. His own pleasure was not something he even cared about in that moment. This embrace was the greatest gift his knight could have given him.

Tomorrow would be different. Tomorrow, Hal would face the Nameless Knight, and Perrin would watch from the sidelines, and perhaps nothing would change between them in the long run.

But tonight, Perrin had given Hal what he needed. And he had proven, at least to himself, that he mattered beyond the function he served.

"You're welcome, Ser Halden," Perrin whispered, and wished his knight would kiss him.

Ser Halden did not. But that was alright.

This embrace would have to be enough.

9
HAL

Hal's shoulder screamed when Perrin lifted the pauldron into place. He'd managed three hours of sleep, maybe less. His eyes felt gritty, his mouth tasted like copper and regret, and every muscle in his body had opinions about the previous night's activities. The ribs on his right side ached where Alaric's lance had caught him days ago, and his hip had decided it was very unhappy about the fall, but he focused on feeling these deep bruises of impact over the mess of emotion in his gut. Physical pain was familiar, a constant presence. He'd been foolish to think other sensations were better than this. Pain, at least, he could trust.

Perrin's hands moved with their usual efficiency, buckling and adjusting, but the squire was unusually quiet this morning. His touch was careful in a new way, tentative where it had always been certain, if overly attentive. Hal hoped that would pass; he didn't want to speak on the previous night. What good would words do? It had happened, and perhaps Hal would like it to happen again.

But only if it didn't prevent his bloody squire from doing his job.

"Tighter," Hal said when Perrin hesitated on the chest straps. His voice came out rough. The squire obeyed without comment, cinching the buckles until the breastplate sat properly. His thin fingers checked each fastening twice, but his eyes wouldn't quite meet Hal's. There was a mark on his neck—just visible above his collar—where Hal's mouth had been after. After Perrin had knelt for him.

Hal looked away. Focused on his breathing, on the weight of armour settling onto his frame. The cuirass felt heavier than usual, or maybe he was just tired. His legs trembled slightly when he stood, too. If it *was* exhaustion, it was catching up with him at exactly the wrong moment. No, damn it, his body would obey him. He forced his legs to steady through sheer will.

The morning sun had burned off the night's chill, leaving the tournament grounds sticky with heat. Sweat already gathered under Hal's gambeson, and he hadn't even mounted yet. Around them, the crowd was building—larger than any day previous, drawn by the promise of a final match between the Upstart and the mysterious Nameless Knight. Hal knew they wanted to know if the first bout had been a fluke. He needed to confirm that for them; he needed to reclaim his title and his glory.

"Your lance, Ser."

Hal took the freshly balanced lance from Perrin and tested the weight. Thirteen feet of ash wood tipped with a blunted crown, capable of delivering enough force to crack ribs or shatter shoulders or end a man's tournament career. Or reclaim one. But as he held it, he thought of the lance that had unseated him days ago. Had it felt like this in Alaric's grip, perfectly balanced, an extension of the rider rather than a separate tool?

He shook the thought away. Couldn't afford to think about Alaric's hands, about where they'd been, about what they'd done. Couldn't afford to remember silver eyes or that cruel smile or a humiliation more bitter than any loss in the lists.

Focus.

His mount waited at the edge of the field. Hal heaved himself into the saddle, his shoulder protesting the motion. Perrin handed up his shield, and Hal settled it against his left arm, feeling the familiar weight distribute across his forearm and shoulder. The yellow-and-blue of Lady Kerran's colours looked faded in the morning light, sun-bleached from too many tournaments. He'd need to request new livery soon. If he won today, she'd probably grant it. If he lost—

No. What was he thinking? He was not losing. He wouldn't give Alaric that satisfaction.

The herald's voice cut across the grounds, announcing the final match. Hal barely heard the words over the hammer of his pulse, which pounded against his throat, his wrists, the hollow behind his knees. Every injury from the past weeks made itself known. His body was a map of small damages, and today he was asking his body for more.

Just one more bout. Then you can rest. Give me this one last bout.

He walked his horse toward the lists' northern end and tuned out the crowd's noise. At the opposite end, Alaric emerged from the staging area.

Even across the field's length, Hal could read the easy confidence in how he sat his saddle. That damned mare stepped high and precise, showing off her breeding with every stride. Alaric's armour caught the sun and threw that glare back, polished as it was to a mirror shine. Everything about him looked fresh and rested and ready, while Hal felt like he'd spent the night being dragged behind a cart for ten miles.

Their eyes met across the churned earth.

That rutting bastard. Hal's grip tightened on his lance. His jaw clenched so hard his teeth ached. Forget the ceremony and the herald's signal! He wanted to charge right now and drive his lance through that smug bastard's chest. Wanted to make him hurt the way Hal hurt, wanted to wipe that knowing smile off his face permanently.

But discipline held. He'd trained to strip his body of the rage, to channel it into precision. He'd beaten better knights than Alaric, whoever he really was. Their first bout had been a mistake.

It wouldn't happen again.

The herald raised his flag as drums quickened to match Hal's pulse. He lowered his visor. The world narrowed, sounds muffled beyond the steel, and there was only this: a rectangle of world where he might change his fortune for good.

The flag dropped.

Hal spurred his mount into motion, driving the heels of his boots against the flank until the destrier surged forward. The lance levelled almost of its own accord, and the wooden barrier blurred past at his left as Alaric thundered up to meet him, his mare covering ground with lithe grace.

In an instant, the distance between them vanished. Hal's mare was slower, but he could use Alaric's speed against him. His lance slid onto its line, aimed squarely at the centre of Alaric's shield, where the blow would transfer cleanly.

Impact.

A bolt of force exploded up his arm. His tip struck true, dead centre, and Alaric pitched backward in the saddle. Yet Alaric's own lance grazed Hal's shield at a glancing angle. It skewed off, force carrying its splinters into the air beside Hal's head, but the strength still wrenched back Hal's shoulder. They thundered past one another, both keeping their seats, yet a thrill pulsed in Hal's chest. He knew Alaric had come perilously close to slipping out of his saddle.

That was Hal's first point.

The crowd's roar crashed in his ears, but all he registered was the steady ringing and the fierce throb in his shoulder. He circled back to his end of the lists, where Perrin waited with a fresh lance. The squire's face was pale but resolved; his dark eyes locked onto Hal's, and he nodded stiffly.

"Good angle," Perrin murmured. "But he adjusted quicker than I'd thought. Watch his left side. He favours it ever so slightly."

Hal smiled. Perrin offered his throat and his insight with the same seriousness. What better squire could a knight ask for?

"Thank you," Hal said, and repositioned himself.

On the opposite side, Alaric accepted his fresh lance with calm assurance. He looked entirely unbothered. Fucking bastard.

The flag rose again. Hal inhaled carefully, counting four heartbeats—five, six—and urged his exhaustion into a taut readiness. This was his element. No one had laboured harder or desired victory more.

The flag fell.

Again. He rode the destrier hard and tracked Alaric's approach, eyes fixed for the slightest tell, and there it was—just as Perrin said, a fleeting hitch in the knight's left arm as he brought his weapon to bear. Instantly, Hal adjusted his grip, angling the tip of his lance out by mere inches.

His lance struck and splintered against the rim of Alaric's shield, levering it back to expose Alaric's torso. The impact was savage and precise. Shield arm splayed, the knight's balance ruptured. He tipped back. For a heartbeat, Hal dared to believe he'd unseated his rival and avenged the days-old slight.

But Alaric's left hand shot out, seizing the saddle horn, and with brutal will, he hauled himself upright. The feat was crude but breathtakingly effective; his mare danced aside under the transmitted shock, but her rider remained.

Alright. Fine. That was still Hal's second point.

That awareness kindled a fire in Hal's chest: he was winning. Two passes, two solid strikes, and at last, Alaric looked vulnerable. The crowd sensed it too, their roar shifting pitch. A frenzy brewed in the stands.

Finally. Things were returning to their proper order, and Alaric's cruelty had failed to rankle him.

He steered back to Perrin, breathing easier despite the pain in his flesh. Perrin's hands trembled as he pressed the third lance into Hal's grip.

"One more," the squire murmured, hope naked in his voice. "One more good strike."

"One more," Hal echoed. A day earlier, and he might have heard Lady Kerran's eagerness in the young man's voice. Now, he heard only true encouragement.

Perrin really was a good squire. Perhaps one day he might be a friend.

Across the lists, Alaric conferred with his borrowed

attendant. Even at a distance, tension coiled in the knight's shoulders. Good. Uncertainty was the least of what he deserved. Trickery meant nothing when lances met; the best knight would win in the end.

The herald raised his flag. This constituted the pivotal moment: either Hal would strike again, unseating Alaric to prove that his first loss had been a fluke, or the other knight would rally, extending the duel until fortune turned.

Hal's grip was unwavering. His breath fell into a measured rhythm. Time suspended. Hal felt his heartbeat slow, the world contracting to the stretch of ground between the horses. Now, or never.

The flag fell.

He surged forward.

His horse thundered forward in powerful strides. The lance seemed weightless, and Alaric was positioning himself for failure—the gap between pauldron and cuirass was ripe and exposed. It was the area Alaric had struck to unseat Hal and that irony had him shifting away from the shield to that tender spot. This would be enough to unseat him.

But at the last moment, Alaric moved.

A subtle lean, a breath's imperceptible shift, and the window closed. Hal's lance struck iron. The clang drove through Alaric's breastplate, shaking him but not unseating him.

Alaric had anticipated it. No. Alaric had—baited him!

Then came Hal's own undoing. Alaric's lance plunged beneath Hal's right arm, angling upward with cruel leverage. He heard something splinter with the hollow crack of green wood and realised only when agony blossomed that the sound was the shattering of his own ribs.

His vision seared white. The lance slipped from his grasp. Reins tumbled through numb fingers. He fell.

It happened in shards of awareness: sky, earth, sky again. The final impact felt detached, as if he viewed another man's ruin. Muffled voices drifted. The armour that once protected now crushed him. Every inhale summoned fresh torment.

At the periphery of his sight, a figure resolved: Alaric, circling back. The knight loomed above, visor lifted to reveal that pale, impassive face. Their eyes met—green and silver, victor and vanquished.

Alaric's lips parted, speaking words Hal could not hear. But no triumph shone in his gaze. What was that he said? What was. . .

Pain rolled over Hal. The grisly landscape of the lists receded as darkness crept inward. Hal's mind drifted to Perrin's trembling hands, to Lady Kerran's impending disappointment.

In that final breath of consciousness, Hal realised he ought to worry about death, not reputation, but he lacked the will.

The darkness felt gentle, welcoming like cool water after a fever. He surrendered to it.

And the world went black.

10
PERRIN

The sound of Hal's breathing filled the tent, shallow and hitching as each inhale caught on broken ribs. Perrin counted the spaces between breaths, his own lungs matching the rhythm without meaning to, as if the sympathetic motion might somehow heal Hal's body.

The medic had left an hour ago. He'd said the ribs would heal with time, if Hal could keep still enough, as if either time or stillness were commodities Hal possessed in abundance.

Perrin sat on the three-legged stool beside the cot, fiddling with his own hands to keep them from shaking. They'd trembled so terribly as he'd stripped the armour from Hal's unconscious body, when he'd felt the unnatural give in the knight's side, when Hal's face had gone grey and his lips blue from the effort of breathing. They'd shaken worse when Lady Kerran had arrived at the tent entrance, her face arranged in what she probably thought was appropriate concern.

Perrin had given her the doctor's account and turned

her away, no matter that she was their patron. No matter that her favour was the difference between Hal being a knight with prospects and a commoner with delusions. Turning her away was the kind of decision that ended careers, but he couldn't bear to have her flittering about, feigning concern. He'd asked her to return tomorrow, when Hal would hopefully be awake, and though she'd looked at him like he'd grown a second head, she'd left.

He had felt like a different man, telling her to leave, and though he'd felt powerful in the moment, now Perrin prayed to any God watching that he hadn't burned a bridge Hal would need.

But he couldn't have let her in to see his knight reduced to this—grey-faced and struggling to breathe, stripped of the confidence that made him Ser Halden the Upstart rather than just another common-born man with delusions of grandeur. Better to feel slighted than to see her broken knight; Perrin would rather bear her wrath than have her drop Hal as an investment gone bad.

The tent's interior was dim despite the afternoon sun outside. Perrin had drawn the canvas walls tight, blocking out the tournament grounds' noise as best he could. The celebration would be happening somewhere—the Nameless Knight being crowned champion, probably. Perrin's hands curled into fists on his thighs. For hours now, he'd entertained the thought of finding the knight and driving a blade between those aristocratic ribs; to do something to make the man understand what he'd done. He wanted to hear him apologise in that cultured voice before Perrin cut out his lying tongue.

The violence of the thought was a new development for gentle Perrin. But watching Hal fall, watching his body go limp in the dirt, had fractured the good-natured part of him.

Hal, his knight, deserved so much better.

He reached out and adjusted the compress on Hal's forehead. The cloth had gone warm, absorbing heat from the fever the doctor said might come. Perrin dipped it in the basin of cool water at his feet and laid it back across Hal's brow. His fingers lingered, tracing the line of the knight's temple, the rough texture of his cropped hair.

Hal's face in repose looked younger. The permanent tension he carried—the set of his jaw, the furrow between his brows—had smoothed in unconsciousness, leaving someone almost boyish. Perrin studied him in the tent's half-light, cataloguing details he'd seen a thousand times and yet could never see enough of: the small scar through his left eyebrow, the slight asymmetry of his nose, the way his lashes were darker at the tips than at the roots.

The knight was too rough for beauty, too blunt in feature and manner, but lying there with pain temporarily erased, he came close to it. Perrin's hand moved from Hal's temple to his jaw, fingers resting against the pulse point there. The beat was steady if fast, Hal's body working hard to heal the damage. Three ribs broken, the doctor had said. They were clean breaks, which was fortunate, and they'd heal straight if Hal didn't do anything stupid like try to joust before they'd knitted. Six weeks minimum before he should even consider mounting a horse. Two months before, he'd be ready for tournament work.

Two months marked the beginning of the next season. His dear Hal would have no time to train, and if he did decide to joust—which of course he would—there was a good chance he'd injure his reputation further when it became clear how his injury had affected him. But if he didn't, if he waited to enter the circuit at a later tournament, then the Upstart's carefully curated mystique—eighteen months undefeated, the commoner who'd climbed to championship level through pure determination—would fade. People had short memories. They'd forget what Hal had accomplished and remember only that he'd been beaten. Twice, now, by the same opponent.

The tent flap rustled.

Perrin's head snapped up, his hand falling away from Hal's face.

The Nameless Knight stepped through.

He'd cleaned up since the joust. His dark hair was damp at the temples, suggesting a recent wash. He wore a simple shirt and breeches. His expression was carefully neutral as he glanced past Perrin to where Hal lay unconscious, but something flickered through his eyes.

Perrin stood abruptly. "Get out." Perrin's voice came out flat and hard; this bastard's breeding didn't matter at the moment. He moved to position himself between his knight and the cot.

"I came to see how he's doing," Alaric said. "That was a hard fall. I wanted to ensure—"

"Get. Out." Perrin took a step forward. His hands flexed at his sides. "You don't get to do this. You don't get to hurt him and humiliate him and then show up here pretending concern."

Alaric's eyebrow rose. "It wasn't intentional. It was a joust. Injuries happen—"

"Don't." The word came out like a bark, that loyal dog in him rearing its head. Perrin's hands curled into fists. "Don't stand there and pretend this was just tournament work. You knew what you were doing. Last night, this morning, all of it. You planned this."

Something shifted in the knight's expression. The careful neutrality cracked. "I—"

"You used him," Perrin cut him off, refusing to hear whatever fresh lie the aristocrat might spin. "It doesn't even matter if I was wrong about your identity: You got in his head, and then you broke three of his ribs. Now you come to gloat."

"That's not—" the Nameless Knight started, but Perrin wasn't finished.

"He could have died." The words came out choked, all the fear and fury of the past hours condensing into his tightly wound voice. Perrin took another step, and now they were close enough to touch. Close enough that Perrin could see the fine grain of the noble's skin, the exact shape of his mouth, all the details that had looked good in candle-light but made Perrin sick in the afternoon sun. "So get out of our tent. Go back to whatever celebration they're throwing you. Accept your championship and your coin and get the fuck away from us."

"Perrin—"

Hearing his name in that cultured voice was too much. Damn it all! Perrin shoved the knight's chest with both hands, putting his weight behind it. The knight stepped back, but he had a well-trained balance. Perrin shoved again, harder, and this time the knight's hands came up to catch his wrists.

The grip was firm, inexorable. "Stop," the knight said, and there was command in his voice now, the unconscious authority of someone used to being obeyed.

"Let go of me." Perrin twisted, trying to break free, but the knight's fingers tightened. They were pressed close together now, Perrin's hands trapped against his, their faces inches apart. Perrin could feel the knight's heartbeat through his palms, steady and slow, completely unaffected by the struggle.

"Listen to me," the knight said. His voice had dropped lower, intimate in a way that made Perrin's stomach twist. "I know you're angry. You have every right to be. But I'm not your enemy."

"You're wrong." Perrin tried to wrench free again and failed. "You destroyed him."

"I jousted him. That's what we're here for. That's the entire point of tournaments—men testing themselves against each other." The Nameless Knight's grip shifted, becoming less restraining and more. . .something else. His thumbs pressed against the inside of Perrin's wrists. "What happened last night was separate. I. . . shouldn't have. . ."

He paused, and Perrin met his gaze.

"I'm not who you think I am," he said finally.

Perrin jolted. "The specifics don't matter. You are some lord, and we are beneath you. You humiliated him all the same." Perrin's voice had gone hoarse. He was still pressed against the Nameless Knight, still trapped by those long fingers, and his body was responding in ways that made him furious. "You're a bastard. A cruel, manipulative bastard who gets off on hurting people."

"Maybe." The knight's expression shifted, something like injured amusement flickering in his eyes. "But not you. You're loyal. Ferociously so. It's. . .attractive."

Perrin's nostrils flared. "I don't care what you find attractive."

"Don't you?" Alaric's head tilted slightly, studying him, before his eyes shifted to Hal. "You were there last night. You saw what I was doing to him, and you saw what he wanted, what he was willing to take from me. And *I* saw how that affected *you*. I bet," he murmured, moving Perrin's collar aside, where Hal's mouth had left a mark, "you came back and gave him something similar."

Heat flooded Perrin's face. He squeezed his eyes shut. He was a squire; backtalking this knight was a death wish. And yet he felt like some feral dog, determined to defend Hal against every threat, real or otherwise.

"My name," the Nameless Knight said, "is Alaric."

The sudden admission made Perrin blink, even if the name meant nothing to him, not in terms of heraldry or local lords. But, after a moment of deep breathing, he supposed it was an olive branch of sorts, a way to refer to the man himself beyond the epithet he'd chosen.

Perrin opened his eyes.

Alaric stared at him, and a lick of concern crept into his otherwise schooled features. "I don't want him permanently harmed. That was never the intention."

"Then what was the intention?" Perrin demanded, softer now. "If not to hurt him, what was all of this for?"

Alaric's grip on his wrists loosened fractionally. "I only wanted to test myself. To prove I could win without my name, without the advantages I was born with. Ser Halden is the best knight here, the standard I measured against—the best fighter on the circuit, truly." His eyes moved past Perrin to where Hal lay unconscious. "I didn't expect to. . . ."

"To what?" Perrin pressed. "To actually care? To feel guilty?"

"To find him so interesting," Alaric finished. His gaze returned to Perrin's face. "Both of you. The dynamic between you—it's compelling."

Perrin scoffed, brazen with his attitude toward this obvious noble. What was so compelling about a squire tending to his knight? What would a nobleman see in them that he lacked in his own life, surrounded as he was by servants? That's all this was, wasn't it?

Except. . .

Perrin turned to look at Hal, whom he loved, and he understood then that was what Alaric saw. Love. A real devotion. Did Alaric lack that from the people he commanded? Did he have anything real?

A kind of petty relief flooded Perrin, then. He may not have been anything more than a squire who would never know a nobleman's riches, but he had Hal. And even if Hal didn't and couldn't love him back, they had something real, a relationship that went beyond what was expected of them. Alaric did not, and no tournament win would provide him with something only true companionship could.

Perrin was playing with fire, perhaps with his own life, and yet he couldn't stop himself.

"You'll never have this," Perrin whispered. "Not so long as you think of people as things you can manipulate."

But even as Perrin said it, he felt something shift in his chest. Alaric's hands were still wrapped around his wrists, thumb still pressed against his pulse, and the touch had gentled into something almost tender. This was the moment where he braced himself, expecting the ire and fury that always brewed in noblemen. Alaric's pride had been pricked, and Perrin expected a storm.

But Alaric only smiled. A real smile, perhaps the first he'd shown Perrin; a sad upturn of his lips, silver eyes full of grief.

"I know." Alaric's voice had gone quiet. "And I'm not here to make things worse. I just—"

"Both of you," a voice rasped from the cot, rough with pain and sleep, "need to shut the fuck up."

Perrin's heart jumped. Ser Halden was awake.

11
ALARIC

The silence after Hal's rough command settled over the tent, even as relief warmed his chest. Alaric exhaled as he turned to see the battered knight staring at him.

Alaric's hands were still wrapped around Perrin's wrists, the squire's pulse hammering against his thumbs, but he couldn't contain the squire once he realised his knight was awake.

"Ser Hal!"

Perrin pulled away and crossed to the cot in two quick strides. His hands found Hal's shoulders, and with a sureness that spoke of practice, he helped his knight sit up.

"Easy," the squire murmured. "Don't try to sit up too fast. Your ribs—"

"I know about my fucking ribs." But Hal let Perrin help him anyway, curling forward in a way that spoke of pain, a body instinctively trying to protect its injured core. His hand pressed against his left side, fingers splayed over where the breaks would be. Alaric watched the way Hal's chest expanded and contracted in shallow movements, each inhale cautious. He grimaced.

Hal's eyes were open. Heavy-lidded and thin as slits, but open. Between his laboured breathing, he fixed them both with a look that settled somewhere between fury and exhaustion. "How long have I been out?"

"Four hours," Perrin said. "You shouldn't be talking—"

"Damn it, Perrin, my ribs are broken, not my tongue." Hal's gaze moved from Perrin to Alaric, who had unconsciously stepped into a half-retreat. "And you. You've got a lot of fucking nerve showing up here."

Perrin wedged himself behind Hal, bracing the knight's back against his own chest. One arm wrapped carefully around Hal's torso—above the injury, so he was supporting without constricting. His other hand reached for the waterskin on the small table beside the cot. Instantly, Alaric felt like the outsider. *Was* the outsider, he conceded; he was intruding utterly. Whatever existed between these two men —loyalty, or love, or that middle ground in devotion that refused neat categorisation—it had roots he could not see and could not compete with. Not that he'd intended to compete with Perrin for Hal's attention. It was only that a petty rivalry could never, *would* never, surpass something like love.

Suddenly, Alaric felt ridiculous. For all of it. For coming here, to the tent, and to the tournament at all.

"Here," Perrin said, bringing the waterskin to Hal's lips. The knight drank in small sips, and Alaric watched his throat work with the effort. Even something as simple as swallowing seemed to hurt. When Hal pushed the water away, he managed to lift his head enough to fix Alaric with a glare.

Those green eyes had lost none of their fire, despite the

pain etched around them. “Still here?” Hal’s voice came out rough as gravel, each word an effort. “Thought you’d have better places to be. Championship celebrations and all that.”

“I came to see how you were.” The words sounded inadequate even to Alaric’s own ears. What had he expected? That Hal would welcome him? That showing concern now would somehow erase what he’d done the night before, the cruelty of his dismissal, the calculated manipulation?

“Well, you’ve seen.” Hal’s jaw clenched, though whether from pain or anger, Alaric couldn’t tell. Probably both. “I’m alive. Ribs will heal. Now, kindly fuck off.”

But Alaric didn’t move to leave. His feet seemed rooted to the floor, his eyes drawn to tracking the way Perrin’s hand rested on Hal’s shoulder, thumb moving in small circles against the fabric of his shirt.

Damn it. He’d wanted this, hadn’t he? He’d engineered his coupling with the Upstart to test himself, to prove he could win without his name. And he had. Only, somewhere in the execution, he’d crossed lines he hadn’t meant to cross. Had let desire override sense when he’d invited Hal to his tent. Had panicked when Perrin appeared, embarrassment and fear of exposure making him cruel.

The memory stirred in him: Hal sprawled and wanting —wanting Alaric without name or title. It had been a gift, though one Alaric hadn’t realised he was aching for until it was laid in his hands: proof that he was desirable beyond the fact of his breeding. Proof that a man could want him without some other game at play. Then Perrin’s narrow frame had cut the light at the tent’s mouth, and panic had seized him.

Why had Alaric done what he had? He’d spent the remainder of the night scolding himself, unsure where that viscous persona had been dredged from. But he thought, in a way, it came from fear.

Perrin's devotion to Hal was absolute; any entanglement with the knight would always include the squire, a truth Alaric had at first wilfully ignored. Worse, Perrin had already come perilously close to guessing who Alaric was. Even wrong, Perrin's natural curiosity unnerved Alaric, who needed to remain anonymous lest he face his father's wrath.

But that hadn't been why Alaric had chosen to hurt Hal as he had. When Perrin had looked at his knight—hurt, shocked—guilt had struck Alaric harder than fear. Who was Alaric to step between such devotion, to muddy love with his appetite? Who was he to take, as he always had, and expect desire without consequence?

Perrin's interruption had laid the ugly core of him bare. He had cast Hal from the tent to save face, yes—but also, he told himself, to spare what was real between the knight and his squire.

And perhaps to flee the terror of how much it had mattered to be wanted simply as himself.

But he hadn't needed to twist the knife quite so thoroughly. That had been fear talking, and panic, and a bit of his father leaking through. His own panic at being caught wanting—not wanting the physical pleasure, which was a thing he could access at any time, but the connection beneath. The way Hal had looked at him with his own desire, like Alaric was worth fighting and fucking and hating with equal intensity, had kindled his heart.

No one at court ever looked at him that way. They saw his name before his face, his title before his worth. Every lover he'd bedded had been paid, or if they were a member of court, had measured what use his favour might be over what ruin his anger could bring. But Hal had seen only a man: a worthy opponent, yes, but underneath it all, a *human*, present, and real.

And Alaric had flung that gift back at him.

"I shouldn't have said what I said."

The words came soft and brittle. What could one expect from a nobleman, without much cause to ever apologise? He floundered, feeling their gazes on him, and eventually cleared his throat. "Last night. What I said about strategy, and—" He stopped as Hal's expression shuttered further. Better to speak plainly, he decided. "I was lying. I'm sorry."

Perrin's eyes snapped to him, sharp and appraising. His hand stilled on Hal's shoulder, but he said nothing. His stare, though, felt predatory; he was Hal's watchdog in that moment.

Hal gave a brittle laugh that broke off in pain. He went rigid, breath shuddering. "You're. . .sorry," he repeated. "About which part? Using me? Or throwing me out like a fucking whore afterward?"

"All of it." Alaric closed the scant distance between them, despite every cautionary whisper in his blood. "I—wanted you there," he began, voice pitched low against the roar of distant trumpets. He hesitated as Perrin's steady gaze pressed into his chest, a living cautery that seared Alaric's fear. He reaffirmed to himself the simplest truth: his bond to Hal was inexorably entwined with Perrin's own unyielding loyalty. If he wanted Hal, he had to court Perrin, too. The admission came with relief and gave him no discomfort, instead sharpening something in his heart. "I wanted it to mean something. And when your squire—when Perrin—stepped inside, I—panicked."

Silence cracked between them like a lance against a shield. Hal studied Alaric as one might examine a rival's lance before tilting—his expression turned coldly appraising, searching for the faintest fault.

At length, Hal said, "You. . .panicked because he made a guess. Because it threatened whatever game you were playing."

Alaric met that accusation unabashedly. "Yes. I came here to prove that I could triumph without. . .certain advantages." He fell silent, leaving unspoken the true edge of his shame and pride alike. "I have my proof now."

"Congratulations," Hal said, his tone an even blade. "Hope it was worth it."

That—wasn't what Alaric wanted. Wasn't what he meant. Alaric felt the weight of Hal's deeper wound: the sting of both humiliations. He swallowed past the lump in his throat. "The joust was never meant to break you."

"And yet my ribs are shattered," Hal replied, voice rough with irony.

Alaric's chest tightened. "I know. I'm sorry." The apology was small, sincere, and insufficient—but finally, he'd offered it. No more dancing around the discomfort. He was sorry for the pain he'd caused.

Hal inclined his head once. The gesture acknowledged the apology, if not its complete acceptance. Alaric drew nearer still, compelled by some secret gravity. "Hear me. I wanted you last night, and I threw you out of fear. You are right: I am noble born, and I am desperate to keep my title secret." He paused, not wholly willing to spell the whole of it out: that their rutting had felt truer than any other he'd experienced, nor that he felt Perrin's love like an all-seeing presence. Alaric straightened and cleared his throat. "When you are whole again, I hope to face you once more."

Perrin drew in a sharp breath, but the squire said nothing.

A faint lift came to Hal's brow. "Why? To finish what we started?"

Alaric's lips curved with a quiet fervour. A flirtation? "Something like that," he said carefully. "To strip away all this messiness and start again. I would meet you purely, on even ground."

"Only the joust," Perrin intervened. Adorable.

"Only the joust," Alaric agreed, though that wasn't the whole truth, either. He craved the clash because Hal was the keenest foil he'd ever known, because in that moment on horseback, rank and privilege dissolved until only mastery remained. Because he yearned to look into those defiant green eyes across the barrier of the lists and know he would not flinch.

But part of him hoped for—and sincerely wanted—more.

Hal paused, Perrin's hand settling on his shoulder like an anchor. Then the corners of Hal's mouth lifted with the promise of a smile. "Alright, Ser Alaric. I agree; we have unfinished business. So, next time," he declared, voice all hard iron and resonant with his oath, "I'll drive you into the earth."

Triumph and relief rushed Alaric, who heard in that declaration a promise he desperately wanted to meet. "Next time."

It hadn't ended, whatever had begun between them. It hadn't ended last night with Alaric's cruelty, nor with his win in the lists. There could be more, between the three of them.

In that shared breath, the unspoken thawed between them: Perrin's steadfast devotion, Hal's hard-won trust, the fragile unity they formed together, and the place Alaric hoped to find, somewhere in amongst it.

Then, to prove to Ser Halden and Squire Perrin alike that he meant every word, Alaric bowed to them.

"It has been an honour," he said. As he rose, he noted the quiet prick of approval tilting Hal's lips, and the sterner, unmoved expression on Perrin's face. *But*, he thought, *it's a start.*

"I should be going," he murmured.

Hal nodded as though granting leave, yet no man amongst them stirred. The invitation remained, quietly ajar. Finally, Alaric pulled himself away, and only at the tent's threshold did he turn. Hal sat pale but resolute; Perrin, watchful and determined beside him. They were a singular bastion, and they intrigued Alaric more than the tournament he'd come for.

"Heal swiftly," he said, voice soft but firm. "Both of you."

With that, he stepped back into the glare of the afternoon. The voices of the tournament swelled in his ears, accolades tumbling in his wake, yet his heart recoiled from their hollow triumph. He leaned a hand against the canvas, chest tight with an emotion he had no name for. A kind of pride, a tender sort of victory, but all of it shadowed by a kind of glee.

He had proved his point. But in that proof, he had unearthed something far more vital.

There would be another circuit, another field. Hal would mend, stubborn and determined as he was. And across the lists, they would meet again, lances levelled, hearts laid bare. Next time, he tried to promise himself, he would not falter toward desire. He would nurture this professional rivalry in Hal, and in Perrin, and with it, he would find himself as Alaric the Nameless.

At last, he turned away toward the dutiful life that

awaited him, though his thoughts lingered behind, counting the weeks until those green eyes would shine across the barrier once more, wondering if his courage could at last keep pace with his desire.

Sunlight broke across his polished cuirass like liquid fire. Behind him, the tent stood silent. Before him, everything was beginning.

Isembard Alaric Blackmere, Crown Prince and Heir Apparent to the Throne of the Sevenfold Realm, Anointed of the Concordant Gods, and Chosen Scion of the Radiant Line, stepped forward to meet it.

THE END

THE BROKEN LANCES SERIES WILL CONTINUE

***SECOND PASS* RELEASES SEPTEMBER 2026**
PREORDER NOW

ABOUT THE AUTHOR

ABOUT THE AUTHOR

Lucien Burr is a writer of dark, sensual fantasy with a background in the Classics and a love for myths, monsters, and morally questionable men. His stories blend lyrical prose, queer desire, and a fascination with power, whether it be divine, political, or personal.

Lucien is the author of **The Teras Threat Trilogy:**

The Teras Trials
The Teras Tactics
The Teras Triumph

The Prince of Lust series:

Prince of Lust
Hell and Its Pleasures
Altar of Flesh
Lake of Sin
Throne of Desire

Other works include:

The Nutcracker and His King

www.ingramcontent.com/pod-product-compliance
Lightning Source LLC
Chambersburg PA
CBHW011225190726
48287CB00008B/2747